**The ferocity of the pleasure that shuddered through her made Kate press herself pleadingly into Sean.**

"You know what happens when you do that, don't you?" Sean groaned thickly.

Her actions were those of the woman she had been, not the woman she now was. That woman had had every right to lay claim to the intimacy of Sean's body, to touch it and caress it however and wherever she wished, just as Sean had had every right to do the same with hers.

"Two can play at that game," Sean warned her, placing her hand against his body.

She hadn't touched a man in all the years they had been apart. Yet immediately and instinctively her fingers stroked lovingly over him.

"Kate... Kate..."

This was heaven and it was hell. It was everything he had ever wanted and everything he could never have, Sean recognized. Hungrily he pulled her into his arms and started to kiss her with fierce, possessive passion.

*Legally wed,*
*But he's never said....*
*"I love you."*

*They're*

The series where marriages are
made in haste...and love comes later....

Watch for more books in the
popular WEDLOCKED! Miniseries.
Available only from Harlequin Presents®

Coming soon:
*Surrender to Marriage*
by Sandra Field
#2443

# *Penny Jordan*

# MISTRESS TO HER HUSBAND

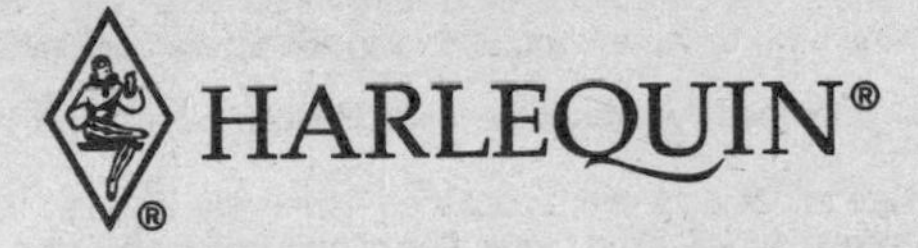


TORONTO • NEW YORK • LONDON
AMSTERDAM • PARIS • SYDNEY • HAMBURG
STOCKHOLM • ATHENS • TOKYO • MILAN • MADRID
PRAGUE • WARSAW • BUDAPEST • AUCKLAND

ISBN 0-373-12421-X

MISTRESS TO HER HUSBAND

First North American Publication 2004.



This edition published by arrangement with Harlequin Books S.A.



www.eHarlequin.com

**Printed in U.S.A.**

# CHAPTER ONE

'KATE you'll never guess what! John told us this morning, whilst you were at the dentist. The business has been taken over. And the new boss is coming in tomorrow to interview everyone!'

Kate Vincent digested her co-worker's excited comments in silence. Dropping enviably thick, dark lashes reflectively over topaz eyes, she considered what she had been told. She had only been with the company for six months, as before that she'd only been able to manage a part-time job whilst she was completing her Master's. With the qualification nicely enhancing her CV she had felt confident enough to apply for this post, which previously she would have considered out of her range.

'So who's taking us over?' Kate questioned Laura, absently flipping the smooth length of her chestnut-brown hair over her shoulder as she did so. It had been hot outside in the street, and the coolness of the office's air-conditioning was very welcome.

'Well, John wouldn't say,' Laura responded, suppressing a small envious sigh as she studied Kate's elegantly slender body, clad in a neat white T-shirt teamed with a chocolate-brown linen skirt.

Laura had been with her when Kate had bought the skirt, an end-of-line sale buy which she herself would have deemed dull. But on Kate it looked not just good, but also somehow discreetly expensive.

'Apparently everything has to be kept hush-hush until tomorrow.' She gave Kate a rueful look.

'I suppose we should have seen it coming. After all, John has been hinting for ages that he'd like to take early retirement—but I never thought he was contemplating selling out. Mind you, he and Sheila don't have any children, do they? So I don't suppose there's much point in hanging on when they could be spending their time in that condo of theirs in Miami.'

Kate listened intently to Laura as she booted up her computer. The business John Loames had set up to supply specialist facilities and equipment to the building trade had been very successful, but Kate had seen for herself since she had started to work for the small private company as its accounts executive that John was growing less and less inclined to seek out new contracts. Which was a pity, because she knew that the business had a great deal of potential, and she was not entirely surprised that someone had bought John out.

'Everyone's worried about what might happen,' Laura confided to her. 'None of us want to lose our jobs.'

'Someone new taking over might not necessarily be a bad thing,' Kate pointed out to her calmly. 'There's ample room for the business to be expanded, and then there would be more than enough work for all of us—provided, of course, the new owner doesn't already own a similar business and just wants to amalgamate John's with his own.'

'Oh, don't say that!' Laura begged worriedly, giving a small shudder. 'Roy and I have only just increased our mortgage so that we can extend the house.' Her face became slightly pink. 'We're trying for a family, and a baby will mean that we definitely need extra space. The last thing I need right now is to lose my job! Which reminds me—John told us that he wants us all here especially early tomorrow. Apparently the new owner has said specifically that he will be here at eight.'

'Eight?' Kate switched her attention from her e-mails to Laura, her forehead crinkling in a worried frown. 'Are you telling me John wants us here at *eight*?'

'Yes.'

Kate's porcelain-clear skin paled slightly. It was impossible for her to make it to the office for eight o'clock in the morning. Pre-school didn't start until eight, and she would have to leave Ollie at seven-thirty at the very latest if she was to make it here for eight. She could feel the tension cramping her stomach.

It was hard enough for any mother to work full time—a constant finely-judged balancing act—but when one added into that delicate balance the fact that the mother in question was a single parent, fighting desperately hard to give as much emotional security as two loving parents would, plus the fact that she had not told her employers that she had child, then that balancing act became dangerously unstable.

Just thinking about Ollie was enough to have her stomach twisting in knots of maternal protective anxiety.

'What's wrong?' Laura asked curiously, sensing her tension.

'Er...nothing.'

Kate hadn't told anyone at work about Ollie. All too sensitive to the attitude of colleagues and employers to the difficulties that came hand in hand with a worker who was a mother—especially a single mother—Kate had made no mention of her son during her interview with John. It had only been after she had started to work for the company that she had learned that John had a somewhat old-fashioned attitude about employing women with very young children. By then she had realised how well suited she was to her job, and it to her, and although it had caused her some sleepless nights and many qualms, she had decided to keep Ollie's existence a secret. Since she was fiercely honest by nature, this decision had pricked her conscience on more than one occasion, but she had told herself that it was a necessary omission if she was to succeed with her career plans.

She was well qualified now, and she was determined to provide her son with at least some of the material benefits he would have enjoyed had his father not abandoned her.

His father! Kate could feel the cold sickness and despair laced with anger spewing up inside her—it was a mixture as dangerous and toxic as arsenic, but she was the one it threatened to poison and destroy, not the man who had broken her heart and deserted her.

Now she considered that she and Oliver were better off without him—even though what she was earning only just covered the mortgage she was paying on the tiny cottage she had bought in a pretty village several miles away from the town and Oliver's out-of-school childcare, leaving just enough for food and other essentials.

Childcare! Her lips, normally soft and sweetly curved, hardened and thinned. *She* was the best person to be providing her son with childcare, but she was not in a financial position to be able to do so.

Her current job was the first rung on the career ladder she was going to have to climb in order to support them both properly. The head of her department was due to retire in two years' time, and Kate had secretly been hoping that if she did her job well enough John might promote her into the vacancy.

Her twenty-fifth birthday wasn't that far away, and

neither was Ollie's fifth. His fifth birthday and her fifth year of being alone, of being without— Swiftly Kate buried the potentially damaging thoughts. She didn't need them, she didn't want them, and she damn well wasn't going to let them disturb her hard-won peace of mind.

It was her future she needed to focus on, and not her past! This takeover could destroy any chance she might have had of such a promotion, but it might also give her increased opportunities, she reflected, as she studied some comparison charts she had set up on her own initiative, to see which customers could be approached to increase their orders.

As she stood in the open doorway of the small village nursery and watched her son run towards her, his face lighting up as he saw her, Kate felt her heart contract with love. When she bent to scoop him up into her arms, and buried her face into the warm flesh of his neck to breathe in his delicious little-boy smell, she knew that no matter what sacrifices she had to make, or how hard she had to work, she would do it for Ollie's sake.

A small frown pleated her forehead as she looked round the classroom, empty now of the other children. She had chosen to live in the village because she had wanted to provide Ollie with a sense of belonging and community, to provide him with the kind of childhood she herself had been denied. But living here meant she had to travel to the city to work, which in turn meant that Ollie had to wait for her long after the others had been collected.

She had never intended that her child should grow up like this—an only child with no family other than her.

She had wanted things to be so different for her child, her children, than they had been for her.

Two loving parents, siblings, the sure knowledge of being loved and wanted. *The sure knowledge of being loved and wanted!*

Pain gripped her. It had been five years—surely only a woman with no sense of self-worth or self-respect would allow herself to think about a man who had betrayed her love and rejected her? A man who had sworn love for ever, who had sworn that he shared her dreams and goals, who had taught her to trust and love him, and who had whispered against her lips as he took her virginal body that he wanted to give her his child, that he wanted to surround that child with love and security.

A man who had lied to her and left her broken-hearted, disillusioned, and completely alone.

To be with him she had gone against the wishes of the aunt and uncle who had brought her up, and because of that they had disowned her.

Not that Kate would have wanted her aunt and uncle involved in the life of her precious son. They might have given her a home when she had been orphaned, but they had done so out of duty and not love. And she had craved love so badly, so very badly.

'Ollie was beginning to worry.'

The faint hint of reproach in the nursery teacher's voice made Kate wince inwardly.

'I know I'm a bit late,' she apologised. 'There was an accident on the bypass.'

The nursery teacher was comfortably round and in late middle age. She had grandchildren herself, and her small charges loved and respected her. Kate had lost count of the number of time she had heard Ollie insisting, 'But Mary says…'

Ten minutes later Kate was unlocking the door to their small cottage. It was right in the centre of the village, its front windows overlooking the green, with its duck pond, and at the back of the house a long narrow garden.

Ollie was a sturdily built child, with firm solid muscles and a head of thick black curls. An inheritance from his father, although Ollie himself did not know it.

So far as Kate was concerned the man who had fathered her son no longer existed, and she refused to allow him any place in their lives. Ollie's placid nature meant that until recently he had accepted that he did not have a father, without asking Kate very many questions about him. However, the fact that his new best friend *did* have a father had led to Ollie starting to want to know more.

Kate frowned. So far Ollie had been content with her responses, but it made her heart ache to see the way he watched longingly whilst Tom Lawson played with his son.

Sean unfurled his long body from the seat of his Mercedes and stood still whilst he looked at the building in front of him.

His handmade Savile Row suit sat elegantly on his lean-limbed body, the jacket subtly masking the powerful breadth of his shoulders and the muscles he had built up in the years when he had earned his living hiring himself out to whichever builder would take him on.

His sweat had gone into the making of more than one motorway, as well as several housing estates, but even in those days as an ill-educated teenager he had promised himself that one day things would be different, that one day he would be the man giving the orders and not taking them.

As a young child he'd literally had to fight for his food until, aged five, he'd been abandoned by his hippie mother and been taken into care. In his twenties he had spent his days building extensions, and anything else he would get paid for, and his nights studying for a Business Studies degree. He had celebrated his thirty-first birthday by selling the building company he had built up from nothing for twenty million. Had he wanted to do so, he could have retired. But that was not his way. He had seen the potential of companies such as John's and had seized the opportunities with both hands. He was now thirty-five.

He had big expansion plans for the business he had just acquired, but for his plans to succeed he needed the right kind of workforce. A dedicated, energetic, enthusiastic and ambitious workforce. This morning he was going to meet his new employees, and he was going to assess them in the same way he had assessed those who had worked for him when he had first set up in business—by meeting them face to face. Then—and only then—would he read their personnel files.

He was an arrestingly good-looking man, but the early-morning sunlight picked out the harsh lines that slashed from his nose to his mouth and revealed a man of gritty determination who rarely smiled. He wore his obvious sexuality with open cynicism, and it glittered in the dense Celtic blue of his eyes now, as a young woman stopped walking to give him an appreciative and appraising look.

In the years since he had made his millions he had been pursued by some extraordinarily beautiful women, but Sean knew that they would have turned away in disgust and contempt from the young man he had once been.

Something—part bitterness and part pain—took the warmth from his gaze and dulled its blueness.

He had come a long way from what he had once been. A long way—and yet still not far enough?

Locking his car, he started to stride towards the building.

Kate could feel perspiration beginning to dew her forehead as she willed the traffic lights to change. Her stomach was so tight with nervous anxiety that it hurt.

She had swallowed her normal pride last night and asked Carol, Ollie's best friend's mother, if she could leave Ollie with her at seven-thirty for her to take him on to school with her son George. The pain in her stomach intensified. She hated treating her precious son as though he was a...a bundle of washing!

Why on earth had the new owner insisted on them arriving so early? Was he just unthinking, or uncaring? Whichever it was, it did not bode well for her future with the company, she decided fretfully.

As she reached the traffic lights she saw the broken-down car which had been the cause of the delay. It was already ten past eight, and it would take her at least another ten minutes to get to work.

Half past eight! Kate gritted her teeth as she hurried into the building. She was already walking fast, and she broke into an anxious run as she covered the last few yards. But the hope she had had that she might be able to slide discreetly into John's office whilst the meeting was still in progress was destroyed as the door opened and her colleagues came out into the corridor.

'You're late!' Laura whispered as she saw Kate. 'What happened?'

It was difficult to talk with so many people in the corridor.

'I'll tell you later—' she began, and then froze as two men came through the door.

One of them was John, and the other...the other...

The other was her ex-husband!

'Perhaps you'd like to tell *me*—now?'

How well she remembered that smooth chocolate voice, with its underlying ice.

People were staring at her, Kate realised, and she fought off her sick shock.

John was looking anguished and uncomfortable. 'Sean, I think perhaps... I am sure that...'

Arrogantly ignoring John, Sean demanded, 'In here!' He was holding the door open, waiting for her to walk past him and into John's office.

For a moment their gazes met and clashed, battled, topaz fighting dense blue for supremacy.

Her ex-husband was their new boss!

How could fate have dealt her such a low blow?

When Sean had walked out of her life to be with the woman he was leaving her for she had prayed that she would never, ever have to see him again. She had given him everything she had had to give—defying her aunt and uncle to be with him, helping and encouraging him, loving him—but that had not been enough for him. She had not been enough for him. The success she had helped him to achieve had meant that he no longer considered her good enough for him.

She was holding her breath and badly needed to exhale, but she was terrified that if she did she was going to start shaking—and there was so way she was going to allow Sean to witness that kind of vulnerability.

How well she remembered that challenging hard-edged blue gaze. He had looked at her like that the first time they had met, defying her to ignore him. No one would dare to ignore him now.

'Kate is a very—' She could hear John about to defend her.

'Thank you, John. I shall deal with this myself,' Sean announced curtly as she walked past him into the room, and he closed the door, excluding John from his own office.

'Kate?' he demanded grimly. 'What happened to Kathy?'

Just hearing him say that name resurrected far too many painful memories. She had been Kathy when he had taunted her the first time they had met, for being too posh to dance with a man like him. And she had been Kathy too when he had taken her in his arms and shown her— Fiercely she pushed away the tormenting memories.

Tilting her chin, she said coldly, 'Kathy?' She gave a mirthless laugh. 'She doesn't exist any longer, Sean. You destroyed her when you destroyed our marriage.'

'And your surname is?' Sean wondered whether she could hear or understand the cause of the anger that was making his throat raw and his voice terse as he grappled with his own shock.

'Kate Vincent,' Kate answered him coldly.

'Vincent?' he questioned savagely.

'Yes, Vincent. You didn't think I would want to keep your name, did you? And I certainly didn't want my aunt and uncle's—after all, like you, they didn't want me.'

'So you remarried just to change your name?'

Anger darkened Kate's eyes as she heard the contempt in his voice.

'Why were you late?' Sean demanded abruptly. 'Didn't he want to let you out of his bed?'

Furious colour scorched Kate's face.

'Just because you—' she began, and then stopped, swallowing hard as out of nowhere the memories started to fill her head. Sean waking her up in the morning with the gentlest of kisses...that was until she was fully awake...and then...

She could feel the tension building up inside her body, a tension activated by memories crowding out the reality she was trying desperately hard to cling on to, to use as a bulwark.

A bulwark? Against what? The love she had once felt for Sean had been completely destroyed, and by Sean himself. Cruelly and deliberately. Her body stiffened with pride. She was glad that he thought she had found someone else. Married someone else.

Had he married the woman he had left her for?

Sean's mobile rang, and he answered it, frowning briefly as he told Kate that she could go.

As she turned to leave Kate heard a female voice saying, quite clearly, 'Sean, darling...'

Kate was halfway through clearing out her desk when Laura came in.

'What on earth are you doing?' she demanded.

'Clearing my desk. What does it look like?' Kate responded tersely.

'You're leaving?'

Kate could see how shocked and dismayed Laura was.

'You mean he's sacked you just for being late?'

Kate permitted herself a thin and slightly bitter smile. 'No, he hasn't sacked me, but let's just say I'm leaving ahead of having him do so.'

'Oh, Kate, no!' Laura protested, obviously upset. 'I can see that things have got off to bad start for you—!' She stopped, biting her lip and looking uncomfortable.

Laura would never make a politician, Kate reflected wryly, witnessing her colleague's discomfort.

'Laura?' she prodded firmly.

'Well, I'm sure he didn't mean anything—to be critical...or unkind. But I did hear Sean asking John where you were,' Laura admitted reluctantly, adding quickly, 'I'm sure he'll be understanding, Kate. He seems such a sweetie, and so gorgeous.'

A sweetie! Sean! Kate suppressed a bitter laugh.

Sean might be many things, but he had never been a sweetie—not even when she had first known him.

A tough, streetwise, untamed rogue male, who could make a girl go weak at the knees and hot in places she hadn't previously known existed with just one taunting look, that was what he had been. And she...

Her face started to burn as she recognised where her unwanted thoughts were leading. She switched on her computer and started to type.

'Oh, thank goodness you've changed your mind,' Laura began, with relief, but Kate shook her head.

'No, I haven't. I'm just typing out my notice,' Kate informed her crisply.

'Your notice! Oh, Kate.' Laura looked aghast, and immediately tried to dissuade her, but Kate refused to let herself be swayed.

Finishing her typing, she checked and then printed off her letter, placing it neatly in an envelope, which she put in the internal post tray.

Her task completed, she headed for the door.

'Where are you going?' Laura demanded anxiously.

'I'm leaving,' Kate answered patiently. 'I've written my resignation letter. As of now, I no longer work here!'

'But, Kate, you can't leave just like that—without telling anyone!' Laura protested.

'Watch me!' Kate answered succinctly, walking calmly towards the door.

But inwardly she was feeling far from calm. Frantically she clamped down on her treacherous thoughts.

Kathy was working here! Sean paced the floor of his office, having terminated the call from the wife of his financial adviser. She had called to invite him to a dinner party she was planning, but Sean did not do dinner parties. His mouth twisted bitterly. Until he had met Kathy he hadn't even known the correct cutlery to use. She had been the one who had gently taught him. Gently rubbed off his rough edges. And he…

He strode angrily over to the office window and stared out of it. He had deliberately not kept track of Kathy after their divorce. There hadn't been any point. The marriage had been over and he had made her a generous financial settlement, even if she had returned it to his solicitor intact. Who had she married? When had she married him?

He went back to the desk and picked up the personnel files he had not yet read.

## CHAPTER TWO

AS SHE climbed out of her car Kate acknowledged that really there was no way she should have been driving. She was shaking from head to foot, and she had no real idea of how she had driven home. The entire journey had been a pain-fuelled blur of fighting back unwanted memories whilst surge after surge of panic and anger had washed through her.

'Kate!'

Kate tried to looked relaxed and smile as Carol, her friend and neighbour, came hurrying towards her.

'What are you doing back so early?' Carol asked, adding teasingly, 'Did the interview go so well that the new boss gave you the rest of the day off?'

Kate opened her mouth to make a suitably light-hearted response, but to her chagrin she could feel her lips starting to tremble as emotions overwhelmed her.

'I've handed in my notice,' she told Carol shakily. 'I... I had to... My...the new boss is my ex-husband!' Tears filled her eyes. She was shaking so violently she could have been in shock, Kate recognised distantly.

'Come on, let's get you inside,' she heard Carol announcing in a motherly voice. 'And then you can tell me all about it.'

Ten minutes later, after she had made them both a cup of coffee and chatted calmly about their sons, Carol turned to Kate and said gently, 'I'm not going to pry, Kate, but if you want to get it off your chest I'm a good listener, and I promise it won't go any further.' When Kate made no response, but simply continued to sit huddled in her chair, her hands gripping her coffee mug, Carol added quietly, 'Not even to Tom, if that's what you want.'

Kate turned her head to look at her, her gaze blank and withdrawn, then forced herself to focus on her friend.

Taking a deep breath, she began to speak, slowly and painfully. 'I met Sean when I was eighteen. He was building an extension for my aunt and uncle's neighbours. We'd had a very hot summer, and he worked bare-chested in a pair of old tight-fitting jeans—'

'Mmm, sexy. I can picture the scene.' Carol smiled encouragingly, relieved to see just the merest twitch of humour lifting Kate's mouth.

'I used to walk the long way round just so that I could see him,' Kate admitted. 'I hadn't thought he'd notice me, but then one night at a local club he was there and he asked me to dance. Fantasising over him when I walked past the building site was one thing. Being confronted with him there in front of me in the flesh was another! I felt intimidated by him.' Kate gave small shrug and looked at Carol.

'I was a naïve eighteen-year-old virgin, and all that fierce, potent hot male sexuality was a bit overwhelming. Unfortunately he thought I was rejecting him, and...' She shook her head. 'I didn't know it then, but like me he'd had a very unhappy and lonely childhood, which had left him with a bit of a chip on his shoulder and a determination to succeed. I can see now that I was a bit of a challenge to him, because I was a girl from a different background. A trophy girlfriend, I suppose the press would call it nowadays, and for a while I was good enough for him as just that. Good enough to marry, in fact. But once he'd become very successful I think he began to realise that I wasn't much of a trophy after all, and that with his money he could afford a much, much better one than me.'

Carol could hear the pain in Kate's voice. 'You obviously loved him,' she said softly.

'Loved him?' Kate looked at her starkly, her emotions darkening her eyes. 'Yes, I loved him—totally and completely, blindly and foolishly I realise now. Because I believed then that he felt the same way about me!'

'Oh, Kate!' Carol sympathised, her own eyes prickling with emotion as she covered Kate's cold folded hands with her own.

Kate swallowed and then continued. 'My aunt and uncle were furious when it came out that I was seeing him—especially my aunt. There was a dreadful row, and it came out that she had never liked my mother, had been appalled when she had married her brother. She told me that if I didn't agree to stop seeing Sean they would wash their hands of me and disown me. But I couldn't give Sean up. I loved him too much. He had become my whole world! And when I told him what my aunt had said he told me that he wasn't going to let me go back to them, to be hurt and bullied, that from now on he would look after me.'

Kate exhaled in a deep sigh.

'We were married six weeks later. Sean had finished the extension by then, and was ready to move on to his next job.'

Carol could see the events of the day were beginning to catch up with Kate and, surveying her friend's exhausted hollow-cheeked face, she stood up and told her firmly, 'Look, you're all in. Why don't you have a rest?

I'll collect Oliver from nursery, if you like, and give him his tea.'

Kate was tempted to refuse. But while a part of her was longing desperately to have the warm, solid feel of Oliver's sturdy body in her arms, so that she could hold him and take comfort from his presence, another part of her said that this was not fair to her son and that she must not get into the habit of leaning on him emotionally. And anyway, she had things to do, she reminded herself grimly. Like finding a new job for a start!

'You're very kind,' she told Carol wanly.

'Nonsense. I know you'd do the same for me.'

She would, of course, but it was hardly likely that she would ever be asked to do so, Kate acknowledged wearily after Carol had gone. Carol had a loving husband, and George had two sets of adoring grandparents only too willing to spend as much time as they could with their grandson.

And Oliver only had her. No grandparents. Just her. Just her? What about Sean? He was Oliver's father, after all, Kate reminded herself angrily.

Sean!

Her whole body felt heavy with misery and despair. She had struggled so hard, and it seemed so unfair that she should have her precious financial security snatched from her because her ex-husband had taken over the company.

For the first time since Sean had announced that their marriage was over Kate felt angry with herself for not accepting the generous pay-off he had offered her. Two million pounds and she had turned it down! She had turned it down not knowing that she was already pregnant with Oliver. And then, when she had realised... Well, she had sworn that she would never ask for anything from the man who had cold-bloodedly told her that he had changed his mind about wanting to be a father and that he had no desire to tie himself to a wife he no longer loved.

The pain was just as sharp as she remembered it being, and she stiffened against it. It should not exist any more. It should have been destroyed, just like Sean had destroyed their marriage.

All those things he had said to her and she had believed in; like how he, too, longed for children. All those promises he had made her—that those children, their children, would have the parental love neither of them had ever known. They had all been lies.

Against her will Kate could feel herself being drawn back into the past and its painful memories.

There had been no warning of what was to come, or of how vulnerable her happiness was. In fact only the previous month Sean had taken her away on an idyllic and very romantic break to an exclusive country house hotel—to make up, he had told her lovingly, for the fact that the negotiations he had been involved in to secure a very valuable contract had gone on so long that they had not been able to have a summer holiday.

They had arrived late in the afternoon and had enjoyed a leisurely and very romantic walk through the grounds. And then they had gone back to their room and Sean had undressed her and made love to her.

They had been late for dinner, she remembered—very late. And during it Sean had handed her a large brown envelope, telling her to open it. When she had done so she had found inside the sale details of a pretty Georgian rectory she and Sean had driven past early in the year.

'You said it was the kind of place you had always

wanted to live in,' he had reminded her simply. 'It's coming up for sale.'

She'd spent the rest of the evening in a daze, already excitedly planning how she would decorate the house, and insisting that Sean listen to her as she went through the house room by room.

They had made love again that night, and in the morning. And afterwards she had lain in Sean's arms, her eyes closed, whilst she luxuriated in breathing in the sexually replete scent of him and wondered what on earth she had done to merit such happiness.

Less than a month later she had been wondering what on earth she had done to merit such intense pain.

One minute—or so she had thought—Sean had been negotiating for the purchase of the rectory; the next he had been telling her that he no longer loved her and that he intended to divorce her.

Kate closed her eyes and lay back in her chair. She felt both physically and emotionally exhausted. What she should be doing right now, she told herself grimly, was worrying about how she was going to get another job, instead of wallowing in self-pity about the past.

She would have to enrol with an employment agency, and then probably take on as much work as she could get until she found a permanent position. She had some savings—her rainy day money—but that would not last for very long.

Why, why, *why* had Sean had to come back into her life like this? Hadn't he hurt her enough?

Tiredly Kate stopped trying to fight her exhaustion and allowed herself to drift off to sleep.

The dream was one she had had before. She tried to pull herself awake and out of it, as she had taught herself to do, but it was too late. It was rushing down on her, swamping her, and she was already lost in it.

She was with Sean, in the sitting room of their house. It was mid-afternoon and he had come home early from work. She ran to greet him, but he pushed her away, his expression not that of the husband she knew but that of the angry, aggressive man he had been when she had first met him.

'Sean, what's wrong?' she asked him, reaching out a hand to him and flinching as he ignored her loving gesture. He turned away from her and walked over to the window, blocking out its light. Uncomprehendingly she watched him, and the first tendrils of fear began to curl around her heart.

'I want a divorce.'

'A divorce! No… What…? Sean, what are you saying?' she demanded, panic, shock and disbelief gripping hold of her throat and giving her voice a hoarse, choked sound that seemed to echo round the room.

'I'm saying that our marriage is over and I want a divorce.'

'No! No! You don't mean that. You can't mean that!' Was that piteous little voice really her own? 'You love me.'

'I thought I did,' Sean agreed coldly. 'But I've realised that I don't. You and I want different things out of life, Kathy. You want children. I'm sick of having to listen to you boring on about it. I don't want children!'

'That's not true. How can you say that, Sean?' She stared at him in disbelief, unable to understand what he was saying. 'You've always said how much you want children,' she reminded him shakily. 'We said we wanted a big family because our own childhoods—'

If he heard the pain in her voice and was affected by it he certainly didn't show it.

'For God's sake,' he ground out. 'Grow up, will you, Kathy? When I said that I'd have said anything to get into your knickers.'

The contemptuous biting words flayed her sensitive emotions.

'Look, I don't intend to argue about this. Our marriage is over and that's that. I've already spoken to my solicitor. You'll be okay financially…'

'Is there someone else?'

Silently they looked at one another whilst Kathy prayed that he would say no, but instead he taunted her. 'What do you think?'

Her whole body was shaking, and even though she didn't want to she started to cry, sobbing out Sean's name in frantic pleading disbelief…

Why the hell was he doing this? Sean's hands clenched on the wheel as he drove. What was the point in risking resurrecting the past? She was easily replaceable. But Sean knew that he was being unfair. She was, according to John and from what he had been able to recognise himself, an extremely intelligent and diligent employee—the kind of employee, in fact, that he wanted. No way was he going to allow her to walk out of her job without working her statutory notice period.

She was his ex-wife, damn it, Sean reminded himself grimly. But this was nothing to do with her being his ex-wife, and nothing to do either with the fact that he had discovered from her records, contrary to his assumptions, she was not married.

He was in the village now, and his mouth hardened slightly. Oh, yes, this was exactly the kind of environment she liked. Small, cosy, homely—everything that her life with her appalling aunt and uncle had not been.

He swung the car into a parking space he had spotted, stopped the engine and got out.

He hadn't told anyone as yet about the fact that she had handed in her notice. Officially she was still in the company's employ…in his employ.

He skirted the duck pond, his eyes bleak as he headed for Kate's front door.

He was just about to knock when an elderly woman who had been watching him from her own front gate called out to him.

'You'll have to go round the back, young man.'

Young man! Sean grimaced. He didn't think he had ever been young—he had never been *allowed* to be young! And as for being a man… Something dark and dangerous hardened his whole face as he obeyed the elderly woman's instructions.

It took him several minutes to find the path which ran behind the back gardens of the cottages. The gate to Kate's wouldn't open at first, and then he realised that it was bolted on the inside and he had to reach over to unbolt it. Hardly a good anti-thief device, he reflected, giving it a frowning and derisory look as he unfastened it and walked up the path.

He frowned even more when he realised that the back door was slightly open. If Kate had had his upbringing she would have been a damn sight more safety conscious!

His hand was on the door when he heard her cry out his name.

He reacted immediately, thrusting open the door and striding into the kitchen, then coming to an abrupt halt when he saw her lying in the chair asleep. He felt as though all the air had been knocked out of his lungs, his chest tightening whilst he tried to draw in a ragged breath of air.

He had always loved watching her as she slept, absorbing the sight of her with a greedy secret pleasure—her long dark lashes, lying silkily against her delicate skin, her lips slightly parted, her face turned to one side so that the whole of one pretty ear was visible. The very fact that she was asleep made her so vulnerable, showed how much she trusted him, showed how much she was in need of his protection…

Without thinking Sean stepped forward, his hand lifting to push the heavy swathe of hair off her face, and then abruptly he realised that this was the present, not the past, and he stopped.

But it was too late. Somehow, as though she had sensed he was there, Kate cried out his name in great distress. For a second he hesitated, and then, taking a deep breath, he put his hand on her shoulder and gave her a small squeeze.

Immediately Kate woke up, and as she opened her eyes he demanded brusquely, 'Sean, what?'

Kate stared up at him. Her dream was still fogging her brain, and it took her several valuable seconds to wake up fully, incomprehension clouding her eyes.

'You were crying out my name,' Sean prompted softly.

Kate felt a prickle of awareness run over her. And then the reality of what she had been dreaming hit her. Her face started to burn. All at once there was a dangerous tension in the small room.

'I was dreaming, that's all,' she defended herself sharply.

'Do you often dream about me?'

The danger was increasing by the heartbeat.

She could feel her skin tightening in reaction to his taunt. 'It was more of a nightmare,' she retaliated quickly.

'You haven't remarried.' He said it flatly, like an accusation, in an abrupt change of tack.

Clumsily Kate got to her feet. Even standing up she was still a long way short of his height. She cursed the fact that she was not wearing her heels, and felt the old bitterness mobilising inside her

'Remarry? Do you really think I would want to risk marrying again after what you did to me?' she demanded hotly. 'No, I haven't remarried, and I never will.'

And there was also a very good reason why she wouldn't, but she had no intention of telling him so. It was her son. Her precious Ollie was not going to be given a stepfather who might not love him. Kate had firsthand knowledge of what that felt like, and she was not going to subject her son to the same misery she had known whilst she was growing up.

'Why did you change your name?'

So he still had that same skill at slipping in those dangerous questions like a knife between the ribs. She wanted to shiver, but she folded her arms instead, not wanting him to see her body's betrayal of her anxiety.

'Why shouldn't I? I certainly didn't want your name, and I didn't want my aunt and uncle's either, so I changed my name by deed poll to my mother's maiden name. What are you doing here anyway?' she demanded angrily. 'You have no right—'

'I've come round here because of this,' Sean said curtly, stopping her protests as he removed her letter of resignation from his jacket pocket, and with it another fat white envelope.

'This is your contract of employment,' he announced. 'It binds you to working a statutory notice period of four weeks. You can't just walk out on your job, Kate.'

Kate's mouth had gone dry, and she knew that her eyes were betraying her shock and her chagrin.

'You...you can't hold me to that,' she began valiantly. 'You—'

'Oh, yes, I can.' Sean stopped her swiftly. 'And I fully intend to do so.'

'But why?' Kate demanded wildly, stiffening as she heard in her own voice how close she was to the edge of her self-control. 'I should have thought you'd want me gone as much as I want to go, given the speed with which you ended our marriage! You can't want me working for you. Your ex-wife, the woman you rejected? The woman you—'

'Rules are rules—you are legally obliged to work your notice and I want you back at your desk so that you can hand over your responsibilities to your replacement.'

'You can't make me!' Kate protested. Her voice might sound strong and determined, but inside she was panicking, she recognised. She did, after all, have a legal obligation to work her notice period, and if she didn't it could cause other employers to think twice about taking her on. With Oliver to bring up she just could not afford to be out of work.

'Yes, I can,' Sean corrected her. 'You may have walked out on our marriage, but no way are you walking out of your job!'

Kate's shock deepened with every word he threw at her.

'I left because you were having an affair—you know that. You were the one who ended our marriage, Sean.'

'I'm not interested in discussing the past, only the present.'

His response left her floundering and vulnerable. It had been a mistake to refer to their marriage, and even more of a mistake to mention his affair. The last thing she wanted was to have him taunt her with still suffering because of it.

'I like value for my money, Kate. Surely you can remember that?'

His comment gave her a much needed opportunity to hit back at him, and she took it.

'I don't allow myself to remember anything about you.' The angry, contemptuous words were out before she could stop herself from saying them. She could feel the tightening of the tension between them, and with it came dangerous memories of a very different kind of tension they had once shared.

'Anything?' Sean challenged her rawly, as though he had somehow read her thoughts. 'Not even this?'

The feel of his hands on her arms, dragging her against his body, the heat of his flesh, the feel of his body itself against her own, was so shockingly and immediately familiar and welcome that she couldn't move.

Somehow, of its own volition, her body angled itself into Sean's. Somehow her hands were sliding beneath his jacket and up over his back. Somehow her head was tilting back and her eyes were opening wide, so that she could look into the familiar hot, passionate blue of his.

Shockingly, it was as though a part of her had been waiting for this, for him, and not just waiting but wanting, longing, needing.

The steady tick of the kitchen clock was drowned out by the sound of their mingled breathing: Sean's harsh and heavy; her own much lighter, shallow and unsteady.

The touch of his hand on the nape of her neck as his thumb slowly caressed her skin sent a signal to her body which it immediately answered.

Now she had to close her eyes, in case Sean could read in them what she could feel—the small, telling lift of her breasts as they surged in longing for his touch, the tight ache of her nipples as they hungered for his mouth, the swift clench of her belly and, lower than that, the softening swelling moistness of her sex.

She felt the hard warmth of his mouth and her own clung to it, her lips obediently parting to the fierce thrust of his tongue—a feeling she remembered so well.

Her fingers clenched into his shoulders beneath his suit jacket as the familiar possessive pressure of his kiss silenced the moan of pleasure bubbling in her throat.

When his hands dropped to her hips, and his fingers curled round the slenderness of her bones, Kate went weak with longing. Soon he would be touching her breasts, tugging fiercely at her clothes in his hunger to touch her intimately. And she wanted him to. She wanted him to so much.

Fine shudders of eager longing were already surging rhythmically through her. If she slid her hand down from his back she could touch the hard readiness of him, stroke her fingers along it, tormenting him, tormenting them both until he picked her up and—

'Mummy…?'

The sound of Oliver's voice from the other side of the back door jolted her back to reality.

Immediately Kate pulled back from Sean, and equally immediately he released her, so that when the door opened and Oliver came in, followed by Carol, they were standing three feet apart, ignoring one another.

'Ollie wanted to come home, so—' Carol came to a halt as she saw Sean, and looked uncertainly at Kate.

'Thanks, Carol.' Kate bent down to receive the full weight of Oliver's compact sturdy little-boy body as he ran towards her, only too glad of an excuse to conceal her face. Picking up Oliver, she avoided looking at both her neighbour and Sean.

'Er...I'll be off, then,' she heard Carol saying hurriedly as she backed out of the door.

Sean stared at the child in Kate's arms in shocked disbelief. She had a child—it was her child; he knew that. She had a child, which meant... Which meant that some other man must have...

Oliver was wriggling in her arms and demanding to be put down. Reluctantly Kate gave in and did so. The moment his feet touched the floor he turned to look at Sean, and Kate felt as though her heart was being clenched in a hard, hurting fist when he demanded, 'Who are you?'

'Ollie, it's bedtime,' she told him firmly, and without looking at Sean she added, 'I would like you to leave.'

'I meant what I said about working for me, Kathy,' Sean responded grimly.

'Don't call me Kathy!'

Too late Kate realised that Oliver was reacting to the anger in her voice. His eyes rounded and he put his hand in hers and stared at Sean. But her distress at upsetting him was nothing compared to the rage she felt when Sean told her curtly, 'You're upsetting the boy!'

To her shock, and before she could voice her fury, Sean bent down and picked Ollie up in his arms.

Kate waited for her son to struggle, as he always did when anyone unfamiliar touched him, but to her chagrin, instead of pulling away from Sean he leaned into him, looking at him gravely in silence before heaving a huge sigh and then saying determinedly, 'Story, please, man!'

Kate felt as though her heart was going to break. Her ex-husband was holding their son, and Oliver was looking at his father as though he were all of his heroes rolled into one. The pain knifing into her was unbearable. She wanted to snatch Oliver out of Sean's arms and hold him protectively in her own. Her poor baby didn't know that his father had rejected the very idea of him even before he was born!

'Oliver's friend's father reads him a story when he comes home from work,' she told Sean in a stilted voice, in explanation of her son's demand.

Oliver! She had even called the child by the name he had… And yet as he looked into the little boy's solemn eyes Sean found it impossible to resent or hate him.

'Story?' he enquired, smiling at him and ignoring Kate.

Oliver nodded his head enthusiastically. 'Mummy—book,' he commanded imperiously, turning his head to look at Kate.

'Please use proper sentences, Oliver,' Kate reminded him automatically.

'Mummy, give me book for man to read, please.' Oliver smiled winningly and Kate could feel her whole body melting with love.

'Sean has to go,' she informed Oliver, automatically using Sean's name without thinking. 'I will read you a story later.'

'No. Sean read Oliver story!'

The frowning pout he was giving reinforced Kate's awareness that her son was overtired, and all too likely to have one of his rare tantrums if he was thwarted—the very last thing she wanted him to do in front of Sean, who would no doubt enjoy seeing her in such an embarrassing situation.

'Why don't you just give me the book?'

The quiet voice and its soft tone made Kate turn her head and stare at Sean in surprise. Oliver was already lying against Sean's shoulder.

'It isn't really his bedtime yet,' she said.

'Is there a law which says he can only have a story at bedtime?'

Mutely Kate shook her head, too caught up in the heart-wrenching sight of her son in his father's arms to protest any further as she went to get Oliver's favourite story book.

Half an hour later Sean nestled Oliver deeper into his arms and told Kate, 'By the looks of him he needs to be in bed.'

'Yes. I'll take him up.'

Automatically she moved to take Oliver from him, but Sean shook his head.

'I'll take him up. Just tell me which room.'

Weakly, she did so.

As he laid Oliver down on his small bed Sean felt the ache of an old and powerful emotion he had thought safely destroyed. Kathy's child. He could feel his eyes starting to blur and he blinked fiercely.

As he left the room he hesitated outside the other bedroom door, and then quickly opened it.

'Where are you going? That's my bedroom!'

He hadn't heard Kate come up the stairs, and they confronted one another on the small landing.

'And you sleep there alone?' He couldn't stop himself from asking the question he knew he had no right to ask.

'No. I don't!' Kate turned her head, not wanting him

to see the expression in her eyes and therefore missing the one in his. 'Sometimes Oliver comes in and gets into bed with me,' she continued.

He had no valid reason to feel the way he did right now, Sean acknowledged, and no valid right either!

'How do you manage on your own? I know you work full-time.' He was frowning, looking as though he was genuinely concerned, and Kate turned away from him quickly and hurried towards the stairs. She wasn't going to make that mistake again—thinking that Sean had real feelings.

'I manage because I have to, for Oliver's sake. I'm all he's got—'

'You mean his father abandoned you?' His voice was harsh and almost condemning. 'He left you?'

Kate could hardly believe the censure she could hear in his voice. 'Yes, he did,' she agreed as calmly as she could, once they were both back downstairs. 'But personally I think that Ollie and I are better off without him.'

She walked purposefully to the front door and unlocked it, pulling it open and making it clear that she wanted Sean to leave.

'I want you back at your desk tomorrow morning,' Sean warned her curtly.

'Well, I'm afraid I'm not going to be there,' Kate responded, equally curtly.

'I warned you, Kate—' Sean began.

'Tomorrow is Saturday, Sean,' she reminded him dryly. 'We don't work weekends.'

There was a small, telling pause, during which Kate wondered what the woman who now shared his life thought about the fact that he obviously worked seven days a week, and then he said, 'Very well. Monday morning, then, Kate. Be there, or face the consequences.' He walked past her and out of the door.

## CHAPTER THREE

'NO!' ANGRILY Kate sat up in bed. It was three o'clock on Monday morning and she needed to be asleep, not lying there thinking about Sean, remembering how it had felt when he—

'No!' she protested again, groaning in anguish as she rolled over and buried her face in her pillow. But it was no use; neither her memories nor her feelings were going to be ignored.

Well, if she couldn't ignore them then at least she could use them to remind herself of how Sean had hurt her. To inoculate herself against him doing so again, because on Friday, when he had kissed her, she had nearly forgiven him…

She could feel the sharp quiver of sensation aching through her body. So her body remembered that Sean had been its lover, she acknowledged angrily—well, her heart had an equally good memory, if not an even better one, and what it remembered was the pain he had caused it.

But the love between them had been so…so wonderful. Sean had been a passionate and exciting lover who had taught her things about her own body, as well as his, and their mutual capacity for pleasure had been something she had never even dreamed could exist.

Why was she torturing herself like this? And if she was doing it then why didn't she do it properly and remember just what it had felt like that first time he had made love to her?

After she had left her aunt and uncle's house—she had never thought of it as home—she had moved into Sean's small flat, but he had told her that he was not going to make love to her properly until they were married. Through the weeks and months when he had courted her he had steadfastly refused to take their passionately intense love-play to the conclusion she ached for, warning her thrillingly—for her—that he was afraid that if he did so she would become pregnant.

'There's no way my baby is going to be born a bastard like I was,' he had said grimly.

He had been reluctant to talk to her about his childhood at first, but she had slowly coaxed the painful truth out of him, and they had shared with one another their dream of creating for their own children the idyllic, love filled childhood neither of them had known.

'But we could use some contraception,' she had suggested, pink-cheeked.

'We could, but we aren't going to,' Sean had replied with that dangerously exciting hunger in his voice. 'Because when we make love, when you give yourself to me, Kathy, I want it to be skin to skin, not with a damn piece of rubber between us,' he had told her earthily.

They had married in the small country town where her own long-dead mother had originally come from—a wonderfully romantic gesture on Sean's part, so far as Kate had been concerned. And in order to marry there they had had to live in the town for three weeks prior to the wedding. The completion of some work project had given Sean enough money to rent a small house for them.

Three weeks was an eternity when you were as passionately in love and as hungry for one other as they had been then, Kate acknowledged. But Sean had made sure that they did wait. He had had that kind of discipline and determination even then.

They had spent their wedding night completely alone in the small rented house. And it had been so perfect that even thinking about it now she could feel her eyes filling with tears of emotion.

'Mummy.'

The voice interrupted her wayward thoughts. Immediately Kate got out of her bed and hurried into Oliver's room.

'What is it, darling?' she asked him lovingly.

'My tummy hurts,' he complained.

Kate tried not to sigh. Oliver was prone to upset tummies. Having checked that he was okay, she sat with him and soothed him, tensing when unexpectedly he asked her, 'Mummy, when's Sean going to come and see us again?'

This was the first time Oliver had mentioned Sean, and she had managed to convince herself that her son had completely forgotten about him.

'I don't know, Oliver.' That was all she could find to say. She felt unable to tell Oliver that he would probably never see Sean again, even though she knew she ought to do so. She had always tried to answer his questions honestly, but this time she could not, and the reason for that was the look of shining anticipation in her little boy's eyes.

By the time Oliver had gone back to sleep she was wide awake herself, her heart jumping uncomfortably inside her chest.

It couldn't be possible for Oliver to somehow sense that Sean was his father, could it? Her little boy couldn't have taken so uncharacteristically well to Sean because he felt some kind of special bond between them?

'It's a wise child that knows its own father,' Kate muttered grimly to herself, clinging to the old saying to protect her from her own wild imaginings.

Apprehensively, Kate parked her car and walked across the car park. The last person she wanted to see was Sean. Why had fate been so unkind as to bring him back into her life? She hated knowing that she was going to be working for him, but, as Carol had pointed out to her when she had told her what had happened, she could not afford to risk him carrying out his threat of pursuing her through the courts.

She nibbled anxiously on her bottom lip as she hurried into her office. Oliver had assured her that his tummy was better when he had woken up this morning, but she had still warned the nursery school teacher that he hadn't felt well during the night when she had dropped him off that morning.

'Kate!' Laura gave her a beaming smile as she came into the office and saw her. 'You've changed your mind and you're going to stay after all!'

'You could say that! Our new boss made me an offer I couldn't refuse,' Kate answered lightly, and then realised what she had done when she saw the curiosity in Laura's eyes.

'He did?' Laura sighed enviously. 'Don't you think he's just the most gorgeously, dangerously sexy-looking man you have ever seen?' she added dreamily.

'No, I do not!' Kate responded, fighting to ignore the sudden backflip performed by her heart.

'Well, if that's true you are the only female working here who doesn't,' Laura told her forthrightly. 'And when you think that he's single and unattached...'

Now her heart was turning somersaults. 'Says who?' she challenged her friend and colleague.

'John,' Laura informed her smugly. 'Apparently Sean told him himself.

Kate wondered what Laura would say if she were to tell her that, contrary to what Sean had told John, he had one very substantial attachment in the form of her son!

Sean was frowning as he ended his telephone conversation with his accountant. But it wasn't his business affairs that were causing him problems. He felt as though he was on an emotional see-saw—something more appropriate for a callow youth than a man of his own age. Moreover, a man who considered himself totally fireproof as far as his emotions and his control over them were concerned.

When he had ended his marriage to Kate he had closed himself off completely from everything that concerned or involved her. He had deliberately and clinically expunged everything about her from his life. From his life, maybe, but what about from his heart?

Nothing had changed, he reminded himself angrily. The same reasons why he had divorced her still existed today, and would continue to exist for ever. Sean knew that he could never alter them. Nor forget them!

Pushing back his chair with an unusually uncoordinated movement, he got up and strode to the office window.

Was that really true? And if it was then what the hell had he been doing this weekend? He did not normally spend his weekends in toy stores, did he? And he certainly did not spend them doing idiotic things like buying ridiculously expensive train sets.

Sean closed his eyes and pushed his hands into his pockets, balling his fists in angry tension.

Okay, so he hadn't deliberately set out to buy the train set. And he had had every excuse to be in the large department store as he had gone there in order to replace some household items. It had been mere coincidence that the toy department was on the same floor as the television set he had been looking at. He didn't really need to put himself through rigorous self-analysis just because he had bought a train set, did he? After all, he had only bought the damn thing because he had felt embarrassed not to do so when the sales assistant had mistakenly thought he was interested in it!

And then he had got rid of it at the first opportunity.

A gleam of reluctant amusement lit his eyes as he recalled the expression on the face of the young boy he had given his embarrassing purchase to. His tired-looking mother had protested at first, but Sean had insisted. He just hoped she didn't think he had had any kind of ulterior motive for doing what he had done. Not that she wouldn't have been right to be suspicious of his motives—they certainly would not withstand too much scrutiny! Dwelling on the past and buying toys just because… Just because what? Just because the warm weight of Kate's son in his arms had reactivated memories from a time in his life that…

A time in his life that was over, Sean tried to remind himself. But the stark truth was already confronting him, even if he did not want to recognise or acknowledge it.

'Fancy going to the pub for lunch?'

Kate shook her head without lifting her gaze from her computer screen. 'Can't, I'm afraid, Laura,' she responded. 'I want to get this finished, and anyway I've brought sandwiches.'

Lunch at the pub with her co-workers would have been fun and relaxing, but as a single parent Kate was always conscious of having to watch her budget.

After Laura had gone, Kate got up and collected her sandwiches. The company provided a small restroom, equipped with tea- and coffee-making facilities and a microwave, for the workforce to use during their lunch and tea breaks. She had just reached the end of the corridor and had started to descend the narrow flight of stairs when suddenly Sean came out of one of the lower level offices and started to hurry up the stairs towards her.

To Kate's dismay her reaction was immediate and intense, and unfortunately a relic from the days when they had been a couple. So much so, in fact, that she had taken the first of the few steps that would put her right in his path before she could stop herself.

Immediately she realised what she was doing and froze in pink-cheeked humiliation as a visual memory came vividly alive inside her head. A memory of Sean rushing up the stairs of their small house to grab her in his arms and swing her round in excitement before sliding her down the length of his body and beginning to kiss her with fierce sexual hunger.

Later they had gone on to celebrate the news he had brought her—that he had secured a new and lucrative contract—in bed, with the champagne he had brought home…

Red-faced, she pulled her thoughts back under control,

'Kathy!' Sean demanded grimly as he saw her shocked expression. 'What the hell's…? What's wrong?'

Alarmed, Kate tried to move away, but Sean stopped her, curling his fingers round her bare arm.

'It's not Kathy any more,' she reminded him sharply. 'It's Kate! And as for what's wrong—do you really need to ask me that?'

She might be Kate now, but Kathy was still there inside her, Kate was forced to acknowledge. Because in direct contradiction of her angry words her body responded to Sean's touch. Was it because no one had touched her since he had ended their marriage that her caress-starved flesh was quivering with such intense and voluptuous pleasure? Was it because it was Sean who was touching her? Or was it simply that when he had kissed her he had unleashed memories her body could not ignore? Kate wondered frantically.

Was it a past need her flesh was responding to, or was it a present one? She knew what she wanted the answer to be! But somehow she couldn't stop herself from stepping closer to him, exhaling on an unsteady sigh of pleasure. Sean was looking at her and she was looking back at him, with the mesmeric intensity of his blue gaze dizzying her.

She could feel his thumb caressing the inner curve of her elbow, just where he knew how vulnerable and responsive her flesh was to his touch—so vulnerable and responsive that when he had used to kiss her there her whole body had melted with wanton longing.

It would be so easy, so natural, to walk into his arms now and feel them close protectively around her. To look into his eyes and wait for the familiar look of hot eagerness darken them, whilst his mouth curled into that special smile he had…

A door opened noisily, bringing her back to reality. Abruptly she stepped back from Sean, her face burning.

Maybe years ago she had not needed to hide her feelings from him—her lover, her husband, her best friend—nor her longing and sexual excitement when he looked at her and touched her. But things were different now, Kate reminded herself as she pulled away from him.

'What's that?' she heard him demanding as he released her and frowned at the box she was carrying.

'My lunch.'

'Lunch? In that?' he derided grimly as he looked at the small plastic container. 'I should have thought for your son's sake you would want to make sure you ate properly.'

As she listened to his ill-informed and critical words, her passionate response to him a few minutes earlier was swamped by outrage and anger.

'For your information—not that you have any right to question anything I choose to do any more, Sean—it just so happens that it is for Ollie's sake that this is my lunch,' she told him, waving the plastic container defiantly. 'It costs money to bring up a child—not that you'd know or care anything about that, since you chose not to burden yourself with children,' she added sarcastically. 'And a packed lunch is a lot less expensive than going out to the pub. What's wrong, Sean?' she demanded when she saw his fixed expression. 'Or can I guess? You might come across to everyone else here as a caring, sharing employer, but I know different. And I also know, before you remind me, that you are rich enough to eat in the world's most expensive restaurants these days. But there was a time when even a sandwich was a luxury for you.'

As she saw his face tighten with anger Kate wondered if she had gone too far, but she wasn't going to back down, and she hoped that the determined tilt of her chin told him so.

'I imagine that your child has a father,' Sean said coldly. 'Why isn't he providing for his upbringing?'

Kate looked at him in silence for a few seconds, bitterly aware of how much he was hurting her and how little he cared, and then told him evenly, 'Oliver's father isn't providing for him financially—or in any other way—because he didn't want him.'

Unable to risk saying anything more without her fragile control being destroyed, Kate stepped past him and hurried down the stairs.

Sean watched her go. Packed lunches, a too-thin body, tension and worry that showed in her eyes. Even if she thought she had it well hidden, her life now was a world away from the luxuries he could have surrounded her with.

Had she thought of him at all when she was with the man who had fathered her son?

Grimly Sean shut down his thoughts, all too aware of not just how inappropriate they were but also how extremely dangerous.

All through her lunch hour, and the two hours following it, Kate couldn't concentrate on anything other than Sean. Her heart was racing at twice its normal rate and she was so on edge that her muscles were aching with the tension she was imposing on them. And the situation could only get worse. She knew that.

Only the knowledge that she had had to protect the life of the baby growing inside her had given her the strength to get through the pain-filled months after Sean had ended their marriage. What was more, she'd had to make the best of it for Oliver's sake. Her love was going to be the only parental love he was going to have.

She had discovered she was pregnant two months after Sean had announced that he wanted a divorce and walked out on her. She had fainted in a store, exhausted by the brutality of her grief.

Until then she hadn't cared if she lived or died. No, that was not true. Given the choice, she would have preferred death. She hadn't been able to imagine how she could go on living without Sean, whose callous words—'You'll soon get over me and meet someone else and start producing those bloody babies you want so much.'—had cut her to the heart. The only man whose babies she had wanted was his. But he no longer loved her. The house they had shared was empty and she'd been living—existing—in rented accommodation, fiercely refusing to take any money from Sean. She had had no idea where he was living. And then she had found out that she was having his child. The child he had told her he did not want!

It was in that knowledge that she had made her decision not to let Sean know she was pregnant. He had rejected her and the pain had almost destroyed her. She wasn't going to inflict that kind of pain on her baby.

She had promised herself that she would find a way to stop loving Sean, and when Oliver had been born she had thought that she had. Until now.

She had to get away from Sean. She had believed that she had stopped loving him, but now she was desperately afraid that she had been wrong. A pain that was not all pure pain, but part helpless longing was unfurling slowly inside her. No matter what Sean might threaten to do she had to leave here, and she was going to tell him so…right now!

Agitatedly she got up and hurried to her office door, dragging it open and hurrying towards the office which had once been John's and which Sean was now using whilst he familiarised himself with the day-to-day running of the business.

There was no one in the outer office, and, too wrought-up for formalities, Kate rushed into the inner office, only to stare around it in dismay when she saw that it was empty.

Or at least she had thought it was empty. The door to a small private room which contained a changing room and shower facilities was half open, and she could hear someone moving about inside it. Someone? It could only be Sean.

Taking a deep breath, Kate walked purposefully towards it and then hesitated, her hand on the door handle. A part of her wasn't ready for another confrontation, but another part of her just wanted to get the whole thing over and done with.

Clearing her throat nervously, she took a deep breath and called out, 'Sean—are you in there? Only, there's something I need to speak to you about…'

In the empty silence that followed Kate began to lose her courage. Perhaps she had been wrong. Perhaps Sean wasn't even here…

She started to turn away, stiffening with shock when the door was wrenched back and Sean was standing there naked, apart from the water running over his skin and the towel he was still wrapping around his hips.

For half a dozen seconds she couldn't move, couldn't speak, couldn't do anything other than stare at him whilst her eyes widened and her face burned.

'Oh. You were having a shower!' Was that really her voice—that soft, breathy, almost awed thread of sound?

'I *was*,' Sean agreed dryly, emphasising the past tense of his statement.

As she fought down the aching feeling that was spreading through her body Kate seized on anger as her main weapon of defence, telling herself fiercely that Sean should have done more to cover his nudity than simply drape—well, not even drape, really, simply hold, Kate decided, before hurriedly dragging her traitorous gaze away—the smallest of towels around his hips.

It was whilst she was doing battle with her suddenly rebellious sense of sight—and coming close to losing—that she heard Sean saying laconically, 'You'd better come in—and close the door.'

What?

She was just about to object, and in very strong terms, when he added dulcetly, 'That is unless you want to risk someone else coming into the office and finding you here with me like this.'

Kate knew there must be a hundred objections she could raise to what he was saying, but as she fought to find one of them Sean reached behind her and quietly closed the door. Closed it and locked it.

'Why…why have you locked the door?' Kate demanded, ashamed to hear the betraying quaver of anxiety in her voice.

'Because I don't want anyone else wandering in here,' he told her dryly. 'Why did you think I'd locked it? Or were you remembering…?'

'I wasn't remembering anything.' Kate stopped him in panic. 'I just wanted—'

He had moved slightly away from her and inadvertently she glanced at him, her gaze held in helpless thrall by the sight of his virtually naked body.

He had already been a fully adult male when they had

met, and she had been thrilled at her first sight of his naked body, her gaze openly eager and hungry to see every single bit of him. She had thought then that it would be impossible for him to be more physically perfect—from the silken strength of his throat and neck to the powerful width of his shoulders, to the arms which had held her so close, the hands that had taken her to places of unimaginable pleasure, the chest so magnificently broad, tapering down to his belly, flat and tautly muscled, with its fascinatingly sensual line of male hair that her fingers had ached to explore.

But she had been wrong! Or had time just done her the favour of allowing her to forget the sexually erotic and perfect maleness of him, her own awareness of it and of him, to save her pain?

An ache at once both familiar and bewildering started to spread out from the pit of her stomach, overpowering her attempt to tense her body against it. A longing that tore at her emotions and her self-control grew with it.

Just above where the towel was knotted she could see the small white scar she remembered so well. The scar was the result of an accident he had had when he had first started working as a labourer, as a boy of fifteen who should have been at school. When he had told her how he had suffered with the pain of his wound, rather than risk being ridiculed by the other men on the gang and also lose a day's pay, she had wept and pressed her lips to the scar whilst Sean had buried his hands in her hair.

And then he had…

As she recognised the erotic path her thoughts were taking, and that it was not so much a memory from the past that was arousing her but a shocking need to experience it in the present, Kate started to panic. She had to get out of here, and now!

Quickly she turned towards the door.

'Kate!'

Caught off-guard by her sudden agitated movement, Sean reached out to stop her. The wrist within his grip felt far more fragile than he remembered. It angered him that she should have so little care for her own wellbeing, and it angered him even more that the man whose child she had conceived had hurt her and left her. The thought of anyone hurting her made him want to hold her and protect her.

Before he could stop himself Sean pulled her into his arms, ignoring her demands to be set free as he burrowed his hand into her hair, unwittingly bringing to life at least a part of Kate's own sensual memory.

'I'm glad you haven't cut your hair.'

The thick, raw words shocked Kate into stillness. She could feel the heat of Sean's hand against the back of her head. And against the front of her body she could feel the heat of…him.

Overwhelmed by her own feelings, she made a sound somewhere between a sigh and a moan, and as though it was the signal he had been waiting for suddenly Sean was kissing her, possessing her mouth with a fierce, driving need and a hunger that her own body instinctively recognised.

There was no past, no pain, only the here and now—and Sean.

His free hand was cupping her face, his fingers caressing her skin, sliding down her throat and then tracing her collarbone.

Hungrily Kate pressed herself closer to him, her fingers automatically seeking the unwanted barrier between them and tugging away the towel. Her actions were those of the woman she had been and not the woman she now was. That woman had had every right to lay claim to the intimacy of Sean's body, to touch it and caress it however and wherever she wished, just as Sean had had every right to do the same with hers. Those rights had been bestowed on one another with love and strengthened by marriage vows.

And though Kate tried to remind herself that they no longer shared those rights, her senses were refusing to listen. They were too drugged by pleasure.

Sean groaned as he felt Kate's eager touch against his naked flesh. It had been so long! Too long for his damned self-control, he acknowledged, as his mouth found the tender hollow at the base of her throat and he buried the sound of his need there, registering the pulse that had begun to beat frantically in response.

Unable to stop himself, Sean allowed his hands to dispose of the layers of clothing denying him access to Kate's body.

Was it Sean who was shaking with pleasure as his hands cupped her naked breasts or was it her? Kate wondered achingly. She could feel the urgent peaking of her nipples and she knew that Sean must be able to feel it as well. When he rolled the tight, aching flesh between his thumb and finger the ferocity of the pleasure that shuddered through her made Kate press herself pleadingly into Sean and grind her hips against him.

'You know what happens when you do that, don't you?' Sean groaned thickly.

In response, Kate took hold of his hand and guided it down her body.

'Two can play at that game,' Sean warned her, but

Kate didn't resist when he placed her hand against the hard, hot flesh of his erection.

She hadn't touched a man in all the years they had been apart. She hadn't so much as wanted to touch a man, never mind even think about it, and yet immediately and instinctively her fingers stroked lovingly over him in silent female acknowledgement of his potency before slowly caressing him.

'Kate…Kate.'

The anguished, tormented sound of her name only added to her arousal, and she stroked him again, moving her fingertips swiftly around the swollen head and down the underside of the thick shaft. The ache deep inside her mirrored the rhythmic movement of her fingers over him.

This was heaven—and it was hell. It was everything he had ever wanted and everything he could never have, Sean recognised as he submitted helplessly to Kate's power over him. But he was too much of an alpha male to allow Kate to take the lead for very long. Hungrily he pulled her into his arms and started to kiss her with fierce, possessive passion.

She wanted him so much, so very much. Eagerly, Kate clung to Sean, waiting…wanting… And then abruptly they both tensed as a phone rang shrilly in the outer room.

Mortified by what she had done, Kate straightened her clothes and fled, ignoring Sean's command to her to stay where she was.

## CHAPTER FOUR

'AND now there's this wretched virus going round...'

Kate pressed a hand to her temple, trying to ease the pounding of her headache and concentrate on what Carol was saying to her.

'It's a really nasty one!' Carol was continuing. 'I've been wondering whether or not I should keep George away from nursery for the time being.'

Through the pounding of her headache Kate tried not to feel envious of her friend for having the luxury of being able to make such a decision. Without childcare she could not work, and if she didn't work how were she and Oliver to live?

After Carol had gone, Kate looked a little worriedly at Oliver. Although he had been playing happily enough with George, he was somehow more subdued than usual.

'Have you still got that pain in your tummy, darling?' Kate asked him anxiously, but Oliver shocked her into silence.

'Will Sean come again?' he asked her.

There was a huge hard lump in Kate's throat, and a pain in her heart like none she had ever known. She wanted to take hold of her son and hold him tightly in her arms, so that no one and nothing could ever, ever hurt him. But there was no point in trying to hide the truth from herself any longer. This afternoon in Sean's arms she had known that she still loved him.

And it was that knowledge that had made her run away from him. He didn't love her any more. He had told her that five years ago. And once it had died love could never be resurrected, surely?

'No, Oliver. He won't be coming again,' she told him gently, her chest locking tightly as Oliver pouted.

'But I want him to,' he said truculently.

Kate could feel her self-control being ripped to pieces by her pain. As she stroked his hair Oliver looked back accusingly at her, and then to Kate's horror asked her the question she had dreaded.

'Why haven't I got a daddy, like George?'

Anguish and despair washed icily through her. How could she tell him that he did have, but that his father hadn't wanted him? He was too young to understand the truth, but she couldn't bring herself to lie to him.

'Not all daddies and mummies live together like George's mummy and daddy do,' she explained gently, watching as he silently digested her words.

'So where does my daddy live, then?'

It was the pounding in her head that was making her feel so sick, Kate tried to reassure herself. But the knowledge that one day Oliver would not be so easily sidetracked felt like a heavy weight dragging down her heart. 'It's bedtime, Oliver. What story would you like me to read tonight?'

For a moment she thought he was going to refuse to be sidetracked and then repeat his question, but to her relief he didn't.

Sean stared bleakly out of the window of the luxurious penthouse apartment he was renting whilst he assessed the future of his new acquisition. On the rare occasions when he had allowed himself to think about Kate ever since their divorce, he had visualised her living in contented rural bliss, with a doting husband and the houseful of children he had known she wanted to have. The reality of her life had shocked him. Yes, she had fulfilled her longing for motherhood—but where was the man who should be there with her, loving her and supporting her?

Sean hadn't forgotten the life he had had before he had become wealthy—how could he?—and he knew her current life must be a hard financial struggle for Kate.

Why the hell hadn't she made at least some kind of financial claim on the bastard who had deserted them both? In Sean's opinion any man who fathered a child should contribute financially to its upbringing. Sean thought of his own childhood—he knew how hard a child's life could be when growing up in poverty. Not that Oliver was growing up in poverty, but it was obvious that his mother was having to struggle to support him.

Angrily Sean pushed his hand into his hair. When he had met Kate—Kathy, as she had been then—he had been an uneducated, anti-social young man with a very large chip on his shoulder. Kathy hadn't only given him her love, she had given him a lot more as well. She had helped and encouraged him in every way she could, and it was because of her faith in him, her love for him, that he was the man he was today.

If only he could acknowledge that debt to her.

He turned away from the window. The penthouse looked like something out of an expensive magazine, and it was definitely not child-friendly. Not like the rectory he had once promised Kate he would buy for her.

Sean closed his eyes and took a deep breath. Had she loved the man who had fathered Oliver? And who the hell was he anyway?

His car keys were on the immaculate kitchen worktop.

It would take him less than half an hour to drive to Kate's cottage.

Sean had made up his mind what he was going to do. He was going to insist that she give him the name of Oliver's father and then he was going to make sure that the man was made aware of his responsibilities to both his son and his son's mother, and that he fulfilled them.

Oliver was in bed and asleep, and her headache had finally dulled. The washing she had hung out to dry this morning before leaving for work was dry and ready to iron, filling the kitchen with its clean fresh-air smell.

Kate liked to do as many of her chores as possible in the evenings, when Oliver was asleep, so that she could keep her weekends free to be with him. The village possessed a small shop, and it was part of their weekend ritual to walk there every weekend to collect the papers and chat with their fellow villagers.

Kate was determined to do everything she could to provide Oliver with a sense of community and belonging, even if she wasn't able provide him with his father.

A shadow darkened the kitchen window, causing her look up from her ironing. She froze when she realised that the shadow belonged to Sean.

A tiny shudder ran through her, the hairs lifting on her skin as she fought against an illogical fear that somehow her own thoughts were responsible for his presence.

Her thoughts or Oliver's need?

She must not think like that, she told herself firmly as she unplugged the iron and then hurried to open the door before he could knock. She didn't want him waking Oliver.

What had he come for? To tell her that he had changed his mind and that he didn't want her working for him after all? Irrationally, instead of bringing her pleasure, that thought only brought her more pain. Pain and a fear that her response to him earlier might have caused him to recognise, as she had, that she still loved him.

Whatever else he was, Sean was certainly not the kind of man whose vanity was so great that he would enjoy knowing a woman loved him when he could not and did not love her back. Judging from his determination to remove her from his life, he would be equally as brutal now as he'd been when he had divorced her.

As Sean strode into the kitchen she just about had time to reflect on how ironic it was that now she was fearing him sacking her when it wasn't long since she'd been determined to hand in her resignation from the company.

'Sean. What are you doing here? What do you want?' Kate demanded, but as she spoke she was achingly aware that what she wanted was for him to take her in his arms and then…

Already a familiar and dangerous weakness was slipping through her veins. He was standing far too close to her—close enough for her to see that he had shaved, and that there was the smallest of nicks on his throat.

Out of the past she could see herself standing opposite him on the sunny street where he had been working. He had been teasing her and she had tried to tease him back, commenting naïvely on his unshaven face. He had looked at her and then he had responded with deliberate sensuality to her comment, telling her that he preferred to shave before he went to bed. 'So I won't scratch your skin,' he had added, watching the bright colour burn her face as the meaning of his words sank in.

A sense of desolation and loss rolled over her.

'Who is Oliver's father, Kate?'

The way Sean was looking at her made Kate's heart turn over inside her chest.

What?

Weakly Kate clung to the edge of her kitchen table as she battled with her shock, wondering wildly how on earth—and, more importantly, *what* on earth she could answer. And then suddenly she knew there was only one way, and that was to tell him the truth.

Before she could lose her courage and change her mind, she took a deep breath and answered him quietly, 'You are, Sean.'

In the silence his face lost its entire colour, and then it burned with a dark tide that swept slowly over his skin until his cheekbones glowed with its heat.

'No.' He denied her words explosively.

His denial ricocheted around the room, burst apart and then bounded back off the walls at her like a deadly missile. Kate's hopes died under its onslaught.

'No!' Sean was repeating savagely, shaking his head. 'No! You're lying to me, Kate. I know I hurt you when I ended our marriage, and I can easily understand why you would have turned to someone else, but no way do I accept that I am Oliver's father.'

Someone else? Kate could taste the acid bitterness of her own anger as she listened to Sean rejecting his son. Beneath her anger, though, lay the bleakness of her own pain. What had she been expecting? Or could she answer her own question more easily if she asked herself what she had been hoping for?

She'd wanted Sean to take her in his arms and tell her that he had made a mistake, that he still loved her. That in fact he loved her all the more because she had given him a son.

'Yes, you did hurt me then, Sean,' she agreed evenly. 'But believe me that cruelty was nothing compared with what you've just done. You can hurt me as much as you like, but I will never, ever let you hurt Oliver.'

As she forced herself to look into his eyes, her own emotion, her own pain was pushed to one side by the strength of her maternal need to protect her child. For Oliver she would sacrifice anything and everything, and if necessary even herself. She could not ignore or deny the fact that her love for Sean had never really died, but for Oliver's sake she would control and banish that love. And somehow she would learn to live with the pain of having to do so.

Everything about Sean's reaction to her information that he was Oliver's father confirmed the wisdom of her decision not to tell him originally that she had conceived his child. But at the same time everything about it tore at her heart until she could scarcely endure the pain.

But it was her anger and contempt on behalf of her son that was glittering in her eyes now, motivating the scathing tone of her voice as she told him, 'That's right, Sean. Reject Oliver just like you rejected me. But that won't alter the fact that he is your son.'

It gave her a sense of almost anguished satisfaction, along with a feeling as if someone was turning a knife over inside her heart, to see the effect his efforts to rein in his temper were having on him. His face once more leached of colour, leaving it looking bone-white.

'He can't be mine,' he insisted harshly.

'Can't be? Why not? Because you were sleeping with the woman you left me for when he was conceived? What happened to her, by the way, Sean? Did you get bored with her, just like you did with me?' Too wrought up to wait for his reply, she threw at him furiously, 'You can deny it all you like, but it won't alter the truth. He is your child.'

Kate shook her head angrily. 'Don't you think I wish that he wasn't?' she demanded passionately when he didn't respond. 'Don't you think I wish that he had been fathered in love, with love, by a man who loved me? By a man who loved him? A man who wanted to share our lives and be there for both of us? You'll never know how much I wanted those things, Sean—for Oliver and for myself. But unlike you I've faced up to the truth.'

She was shaking from head to foot, Kate recognised, and she was humiliatingly close to tears.

For a minute Sean was too shocked by Kate's angry and contemptuous outburst to make any response. And then for a minute more he discovered that he actually wanted to be able to believe her. She was certainly doing a good job of believing herself, he recognised cynically. But all the cynicism in the world could not wipe away the strength of his immediate response to her emotional outburst. Pain, anger and unbelievably longing tore at him in equal proportions.

What had happened to the self-control he had been so proud of? And what had happened to the honesty that had been such a strong part of Kate's personality? Obviously it was something else for him to mourn, along with his other losses. It took him far too long to suppress his instinctive urge to go to her and take hold of her, but eventually he managed to do so, instead telling her brutally, 'You're wasting your breath. There's no point in any of this. Oliver is not my child.' He hesitated, deliberately turning away from Kate so that she would not see his expression. 'And nothing you can say will ever make me acknowledge him as such.'

Kate stared at him, angry colour burning her skin, her mouth compressing, but before she could say anything, Sean demanded harshly, 'For God's sake, Kate, don't make it even worse than it has to be. I can just accept that you gave yourself to someone else after our marriage was over. I can even accept that if you gave yourself to someone else as an act of retribution against me, and that I deserved such an action, but I damn well can't accept that you slept with someone else whilst we were still together.'

'You mean like you did?' Kate shot at him bitingly. 'What happened to her, Sean?'

'She isn't in my life any more. It was just a short-lived fling.'

He sounded more irritated than concerned, and his response added further fuel to Kate's anger.

'Clever her! She must have realised that ultimately you'd probably betray her, just like you did me.'

Sean gave her a bitter look. 'When it comes to betrayal, you outclass me, Kate. You've committed the worst betrayal of all in trying to pretend that another man's child is mine!'

Kate's face burned with anger. 'I would never stoop to that kind of deceit,' she stormed furiously. 'I can't bear to think of what you've done—not just to me but more importantly to Oliver! You've denied your child the right to know his father and—'

Angrily Sean reached out and took hold of her wrist. 'Oliver is not my child!'

The harsh words echoed round the small kitchen, causing Kate to try and pull away. 'I hate you, Sean,' she told him passionately. 'You don't know how much

I wish I'd never met you, how much I hate myself for letting you—'

'Letting me what?' Sean stopped her.

Kate could feel the hard bite of his fingers in the soft flesh of her upper arms as he dragged her body against the hard tense length of him.

'Letting me make you feel like this?'

His mouth possessed hers, its pressure bending her head back and making her arch her spine. Anger and pride mingled turbulently inside her as longing streaked scarlet trails of danger through her veins. She could feel the fierce judder of reaction galvanise Sean's body, and somehow, shockingly, immediately and against all logic, she was swept back to another time and another kiss.

A time when they had virtually only just met, and a kiss had been taken fiercely from her in the concealing darkness when Sean had walked her home from their first real date.

Then her body had thrilled with shocked and excited pleasure at its recognition of his predatory male passion. She had been young; naïve, but oh, so very, very passionately in love with Sean, and so very eager and aroused.

Now she was…

But where did then end and now begin? Kate wondered with dizzy fatality as the years rolled back and her body, her senses, her emotions were those of that young girl again.

Kate heard the small whimper escaping her lips. Instantly the hot, hard pressure of Sean's mouth caught and answered it. His hands moved from her arms to her back, no longer constraining her but caressing her, as though something in that sound she had made had been a plea and not a protest.

She trembled as his hands cinched her waist, his

thumbs caressing its narrow curve, before sliding lower to cup the rounded flesh of her behind and then urge her even more closely against his own body, holding her tight and hard against the obvious thrust of his erection. Automatically and instinctively Kate tilted her hips hungrily against him and moaned his name.

As she sobbed her arousal and need against his lips Kate felt his hand move to her breast.

She was lost to time and place, to everything but Sean and her need for him. A sound, a high, hot, female-hungry-for-her-mate sound of raw sexual hunger slit the thickness of air, which was filled with the raggedness of breath exhaled in mutual passion.

And Sean responded to it as though a door had swung open, admitting him to a lost and long-sought magic kingdom.

Kate trembled as the hand he had raised to her breast began to stroke and then massage it with familiar intimacy, arousing an equally familiar sensation which spread from his touch through her stomach to the soft warmth within her. A soft warmth that was rapidly turning into a tight, wet, aching heat.

Unable to stop herself from answering the clamouring need, Kate arched her whole body against his touch, moaning into his mouth as his hand cupped her breast and his thumb and finger started to pluck sensually at the hard peak of her nipple.

In a heartbeat of brief lucidity Kate was shockingly aware that just the feel of his erection straining against her was as erotically arousing as if she had still been a virginal teenager. But then Sean groaned, tugging fiercely at her top, and she watched him tense as the pale, soft nakedness of her breast, with the ripe swollen peak of her nipple, was revealed to his sight and his touch. Her lucidity became a thing of the past, to be overwhelmed, overturned by the flash-flood of her own response.

Would Sean remember how much she had liked to feel him stroke the hard flesh of her aroused nipples with his fingertip? How it had made her call out to him in shocked, excited arousal? Would he remember the way he had driven her beyond the boundaries of her self-control with the slow touch of his mouth?

She quivered as she felt his hand on her naked breast—waiting, yearning, needing.

'Kathy…'

The raw sound of her name seemed to have been dredged up from somewhere deep and hidden inside Sean, and Kate tensed immediately in response to it.

Kathy! But she wasn't Kathy any more. She was Kate. She was Kate—and Sean wasn't the man who loved her, he was the man who had betrayed her! The man who refused to accept that he had fathered her child. Sickness rolled through her. How could she feel the way she had, behave the way she had, when she knew…?

She froze as the kitchen door was pushed open and she saw Oliver standing staring at them.

## CHAPTER FIVE

SEAN'S reaction had been quicker than hers, and to her shock Kate realised that she was looking at her son from behind Sean's sheltering body. Hot-faced with shock and guilt, she straightened her clothes and moved to go to Oliver, but he was oblivious to her, instead heading straight for Sean.

Frantically Kate tried to stop him, unable to bear the rejection her little boy was going to suffer, but to her disbelief Sean stepped past her, scooping Oliver up as her son held out his arms to him.

Holding Kate's child in his arms, Sean felt a pain like none other he had ever experienced—not even when his mother had left him, not even when he had heard that he could not father a child himself, not even when he had locked Kate out of his life, he acknowledged as he fought down his own anguish and torment.

The small head tilted back and solemn eyes looked into his. Sean felt as though someone had slid a knife into his ribs poisoned with longing, jealousy and despair. Longing for Oliver to be his; jealousy because Kate had given herself to another man; despair because of the situation he was now in.

Abruptly he thrust Oliver into Kate's waiting arms and turned towards the back door.

As he reached it he stopped and turned round, shadows cloaking the pain in his eyes as he demanded, 'When was he born?'

Kate tightened her arms around Oliver, who had already fallen back to sleep, in the way that small children could in just a few seconds, and she told him the date.

After the smallest of pauses, Sean grated, 'So he was conceived two weeks after we separated, then?'

The air in the kitchen felt so heavy and sour with the weight of their combined emotions that Kate felt as though it might choke her.

'He was two weeks overdue.' She answered Sean's unspoken accusation despairingly. Shaking her head, she added huskily, 'They wanted to induce me but I asked them to wait. I…I wanted him to be born naturally.'

Kate closed her eyes and turned away, not wanting to be reminded that she had held out until the last possible minute, clinging desperately and stubbornly to her hope that there would be a miracle and that somehow Sean would be there with her to witness the birth of their child.

But he hadn't been, and in the end there had been no one other than the hospital staff to share her awed and exhausted delight at the birth of her son.

She came out of her reverie to hear the back door closing. Sean had left. But he had already left her life and Oliver's a long time ago, she reminded herself.

Somehow that reminder wasn't as comforting as it should have been. Her pain was too sharp and strong to be so easily soothed.

She could, of course, have challenged Sean to let her prove that Oliver was his son by demanding a DNA test. Kate dropped her cheek onto Oliver's soft springy curls. But proving that Sean was Oliver's father would mean nothing if Sean refused to be that father. No way was she going to expose Oliver to that kind of pain—not even to prove to Sean that she had not, as he had accused, shared her body with another man as he had shared his with another woman!

The pain hadn't changed at all. It was still as strong as it had always been. Where was her pride? Why wasn't it rescuing her from her own vulnerability by reminding her of what Sean had done? How dared he make accusations regarding her when he had told her openly that he had taken another woman to bed?

Oliver was still asleep in her arms, which meant that she did not have to hold back any longer the slow, painful tears burning the back of her eyes. It hadn't just been her that Sean had betrayed, he had betrayed Oliver as well!

Sean grimaced as he accidentally nicked his skin, and put down his razor. 'It's your own damned fault,' he muttered to his reflection as he stanched the small wound. But it wasn't the cut he was talking about, and it wasn't his own face he could see in the mirror—it was Oliver's.

Cursing, he tried to banish his thoughts—but it was too late.

He had seen in Kate's eyes just how she felt about his refusal to accept that Oliver was his child. But no matter how much she had managed to persuade herself that Oliver was his, Sean knew that he could not be.

And he knew for a very good reason.

He closed his eyes and swallowed against the sick taste of his own self-loathing and humiliation.

That reason was that it was medically impossible for him to father a child.

He hadn't known that when he had married Kate, of course. If he had done then he would never have married her, knowing how important having children was to her.

He thought back to the medical appointment which had been responsible for the destruction of his marriage and his life.

'There is one thing I do have to mention,' the doctor had begun. 'One of the tests we ran was a sperm count. I'm afraid I have to tell you that it's highly unlikely you will be able to father a child.'

Even now he still had bad dreams about those words and that meeting with his doctor at which the announcement had been made.

He hadn't been able to take it in at first. How could it not be possible for him to father a child? He was a fit, healthy man in the prime of life. He had protested that the doctor must be wrong, that there must be some mistake, and all the time he had been aware of the humiliating pity in the other man's eyes as he shook his head. The doctor might be twenty years his senior, small, balding, and with a paunch, but suddenly he had become the one who was the virile potent male whilst Sean had been reduced to a mere pathetic apology for a man, at least in his own eyes.

Real men, in the culture of the rough, fight-to-survive world in which Sean had grown up, were not unable to father children.

Inside his head Sean had heard a brief snatch of stored conversation, between his mother and one her friends. They had been talking about a man they both knew, and Sean could remember the mockery in his mother's laughter as she had told her friend, 'He's a poor thing, by all accounts. Hasn't fathered a child yet, nor likely to, and in my book that means he isn't a man at all.'

Not a man at all—just like him.

Another memory surfaced.

'Oh, Sean, I just can't wait for us to have children.'

Now it was Kate's voice haunting him, and he swore savagely beneath his breath.

'I'd hate to have the kind of marriage that didn't include a family, like my aunt and uncle's.'

He could still see the way she had shuddered, as though in revulsion.

'Don't worry, I'll give you as many as you want,' he had boasted, already aroused at the thought of how he would give her the children they both wanted so much.

And each and every time he had made love with her that feeling had been there, that surge of atavistic male pride in the knowledge that he had the power to create a new life within her.

Only he had not had that power. Not according to what his doctor had told him.

It hadn't been just his present and his future the doctor's words had destroyed; it had been his own belief and pride in himself as well. Suddenly he was not the man he had always thought himself to be. Suddenly he was not, in his own opinion, very much of a man at all.

Holding Oliver had brought back with savage intensity all that he could never have, and yet he couldn't hate the little boy—far from it, in fact. Instead of wanting to reject the child another man had given the woman he loved, he had actually felt drawn towards him.

If only Kate knew just how much he wished that Oliver *was* his child! And Kate herself still his wife?

After she had betrayed him by sleeping with another man? A bitter smile twisted Sean's lips.

Kate might have thought that hurling his infidelity at him was a powerful weapon, but instead it was just his own lie to her. His supposed affair had been a lie, made up to expedite the speedy ending of their marriage so that he could set Kate free.

And since the reason he'd been so grimly determined to set her free had been so that she could find another man to father the children he knew were so important to her, it was illogical for him to feel the way he did about the fact that she had done so.

Whoever the man was, he was a fool as well as a scoundrel for abandoning Kate and his son—and for throwing away Kate's love.

The savagery and immediacy of his own pain felt like a hammer-blow against his heart.

'Everyone's surprised that our new boss is spending so much time here,' Laura confided chattily to Kate on Thursday, as she came into her office shortly after lunch. 'I mean, he has two other companies. Do you suppose it means that we can all stop worrying about being made redundant?' she asked hopefully. 'I mean, if he wasn't planning on keeping this place going he wouldn't be spending so much time here, would he? Kate?' she prompted when Kate didn't make any response. 'Other things on your mind?' Laura guessed.

'Sorry—I didn't get much sleep last night,' Kate answered. It was the truth after all.

'You do look a bit peaky,' Laura acknowledged as she studied her.

Peaky! Kate grimaced to herself. She felt as though her emotions had been ripped apart and devoured by a pack of scavengers, and that now all that was left of them was the dead bones.

It was the dry grittiness of her eyes that made her want to blink, not something stupid like crying, she assured herself fiercely. After all, she had done enough of that during the night, hadn't she? With her face buried in her pillow so that she wouldn't wake Oliver.

She was still in shock, Kate admitted to herself, and the cause of that shock was her discovery of just how vulnerable she still was to Sean!

'Oh, no! Look at the time! I'd better go.' Kate hurried past Laura as she made her exit.

Behind her shock and pain lay a huge, deep dam of pent-up anger. How dared Sean refuse to believe that Oliver was his child? How dared he be such a hypocrite as to accuse her of sleeping with someone else?

Thinking of her son made her turn anxiously to her silent mobile. Oliver had complained that his tummy hurt again at breakfast time, but to her relief when she had taken his temperature it had been normal and so she had taken him to school.

Sean drummed his fingers irritably on his desk. Pushing back his chair, he stood up, raking his hair with one hand, and paced the floor as he mentally practised what he intended to say to Kate.

Halfway through the carefully chosen words he stopped abruptly and asked himself angrily what the hell was wrong with him. All he had to say to Kate was that he wanted her to have the money she had refused to accept when they had divorced. Hell, if need be he could tell her that his accountants were insisting it was handed over otherwise he would invoke some kind of tax penalty. His decision had nothing whatsoever to do with Oliver, other than the fact that he hated seeing Kate have to struggle—especially when she had a small child to support.

A small child who wasn't his.

Opening his office door, he instructed his secretary to tell Kate he wanted to see her.

'Jenny rang down to say that you wanted to see me?'

'Yes, I do,' Sean confirmed, turning away to look out of his office window. 'You must have found it hard to make time to study for your Master's?'

'Yes, in some ways I did,' Kate agreed warily, wondering why he had sent for her and what this was leading up to.

'I imagine that it would have been difficult with Oliver,' Sean pressed her.

'Yes, it was,' Kate confirmed.

'Why didn't you ask his father for financial support?'

When she didn't answer, Sean swung round. The light streaming in through the large window highlighted the tension in his face, and for a moment Kate almost weakened. He had been everything to her after all. As she was now everything to Oliver, she reminded herself immediately, before taking a deep breath and asking sharply, 'What are you trying to do? Trap me? You're wasting your time, Sean. *You* are Oliver's father. Nothing and no one—not even you—can alter that fact.'

Her stomach churned as she saw Sean's expression hardening with rejection.

'You are the one who is wasting your time, Kate. Oliver is not my son. He can't be—' Sean tensed and stopped speaking, taking a deep breath before he continued tersely, 'He can't be foisted off on me!'

His heart was hammering against his ribs. It was a sign of the effect Kate was having on him that he had come so close to blurting out the truth! Fortunately he had just managed to stop himself in time!

Kate clenched her hands as she caught the underlying

and suppressed violence in Sean's voice, her dismay giving way to shock as she heard him adding grimly, 'What I wanted to talk to you about was—' He stopped speaking as the abrupt shrill of Kate's mobile cut across his words. Red-faced, she fished it out of her bag, her embarrassment forgotten as she saw that the call was from Oliver's nursery.

'He's been sick and he's asking for me?' Kate couldn't keep the anxiety out of her voice as she repeated what the other woman was telling her. 'He wasn't very well this morning,' she admitted. 'But he didn't have a temperature then…'

Even though Kate tried to turn away from Sean she knew that he could hear the conversation she was having with the nursery school teacher.

'I…I'll try to—' she began, only to find that Sean was spinning her round to face him.

His expression was grim as he took the mobile from her and said tersely into it, 'She's on her way.'

'You have no right—' Kate said angrily, but Sean had ended the call and his hand was on her arm, urging her towards the door.

'We'll go in my car,' he told her. 'For one thing we'll get there faster, and for another you'll be worrying too much to drive safely.'

Kate opened her mouth to protest, but they were already in the car park and heading for Sean's car. He held the passenger door open for her and reluctantly she got in.

'Did the nursery say exactly what's wrong with him? Have they called a doctor?' Sean asked as he slid into the driver's seat and started the engine.

Kate wanted to refuse to tell him anything—after all, he had just rejected Oliver—but her maternal anxiety overruled her pride, and apprehensively she began to repeat what she had been told. 'He's been sick, apparently. There's a bug going round. He said this morning that his tummy was hurting him.'

'You sent him to nursery, knowing that he wasn't well?'

Kate could hear the criticism and disbelief in Sean's voice.

'Why didn't you stay at home with him?'

Angrily Kate defended herself. 'I have to work, remember? Anyway, I can't just take time off like that.'

'Of course you can,' Sean contradicted her flatly. 'You're a mother. People would understand.'

'No one at work knows about Oliver,' Kate admitted abruptly, deliberately turning her head to face the window so that he couldn't see her expression.

'Ashamed of him?'

'No!' Kate denied furiously, and immediately turned to look at him. She realised too late that Sean had deliberately provoked her, knowing what her reaction would be.

'Then why?'

'For goodness' sake, Sean, surely I don't have to tell you the business facts of life?' Kate answered wryly. 'Not all firms will take on women who are mothers, especially if they are single mothers. I needed this job. I didn't mention Oliver at my first interview, and then after I had been offered the job I discovered that John had an unwritten rule about not employing mothers of young children.'

'A rule it would be unlawful for him to try to enforce,' Sean pointed out. 'And Oliver needs you! Hell, Kate, both you and I know what it's like to grow up without a mother.'

'Oliver has a mother.'

'But not a mother who can be there for him when he needs her.'

Kate couldn't maintain her barriers against the pain that swamped her. It invaded every nerve-ending and tore at her heart.

'Since you refuse to accept that Oliver is your child, you hardly have the right to tell me how to bring him up, do you?' she challenged him bitterly, only realising as she managed to blink away her angry tears that they had reached the village.

The moment Sean pulled up outside the nursery Kate was reaching for the car's door handle, throwing a stiff, 'Thank you for the lift,' to him over her shoulder.

But to her consternation Sean was already out of the car and opening her door, announcing curtly, 'I'm coming in with you.'

'I don't want you to,' Kate protested.

'Oliver might need to see a doctor,' Sean told her flatly. 'I can run you there.'

A doctor? Anxiously Kate hurried towards the nursery, her concern for her son far more important right now than arguing with Sean.

The moment Kate pushed open the door Oliver's nursery teacher came hurrying towards her.

'Where's Oliver? How is he?' Kate demanded frantically as she scanned the room anxiously, unable to see her son amongst the throng of children in the room.

'He's fine, but he's asleep.'

'Asleep? But—' Kate began, only to be interrupted.

'Has he seen a doctor?' Sean demanded sharply.

It irritated Kate a little to see the immediacy with which the older woman responded to Sean's calm authority.

'I'm a trained nurse,' she informed him, almost defensively. 'I don't think there's anything seriously wrong. Oliver felt poorly before lunch, and then he was sick afterwards, but he seems fine now—if rather tired.'

Turning to look at Kate, she added, slightly reprovingly, 'He seems upset about something, and I do rather think that might be the cause of the problem. Young children often react with physical symptoms to emotional stress.'

Kate flushed sensitively, sure that she could hear a note of criticism in the other woman's voice.

'I'll go through and get Ollie and take him home,' Kate told her quietly, unaware of the way Sean was watching her reaction to the older woman's remarks.

Oliver was asleep in one of the beds in a room off the playroom, and Kate felt the familiar pull on her emotions as she leaned over him. In so many ways he was Sean's son, even if Sean himself refused to accept Ollie as his child. Tiredly she bent to pick him up.

'I'll take him.'

Kate turned round. She hadn't realised that Sean had followed her into the small shadowy room.

'There's no need,' she told him in a small clipped voice, focusing her gaze not on Sean's face but on one dark-suited shoulder. A big mistake, she recognised achingly, when she had to suppress a longing to lean her head against its comforting strength and feel Sean's arms come round her, hear Sean's voice telling her that he believed her and that he loved her, that right now this very minute he was going to take both her and Oliver home with him.

As she stood there, staring fixatedly at his shoulder, Kate was suddenly overwhelmed by the searing knowledge of how alone and afraid she sometimes felt. Her throat ached and so did her head, shocked nausea was churning her stomach, and just the sight of Sean lifting his sleeping son into his arms was enough to make her feel as though her heart was breaking.

Get a grip, Kate advised herself sharply. This kind of emotion was a luxury she simply could not afford.

Once they were outside the nursery Kate stood in front of Sean and demanded, 'Give him to me now. I can carry him home from here.'

'You carry him? You look as though you can barely carry yourself,' Sean told her bluntly.

'I'll carry him!'

They had just reached the cottage when Oliver woke up, stirring sleepily in Sean's arms.

Opening the door, Kate stood just inside it and held out her arms for her son. But to her chagrin Oliver turned away from her, burrowing his head against Sean's chest and going back to sleep.

A huge splinter of ice was piercing her heart. This was the first time Oliver had rejected her in favour of someone else—and not just anyone else, but Sean, his father.

'You'd better give him to me,' she told Sean sharply. 'I'm sure the last thing you'll want is him being sick on your suit.'

As he handed Oliver to her and she put him down gently on the shabby sofa that took up one wall of the kitchen she heard him say quietly, 'No, actually the last thing I want is knowing that you went to another man's bed so quickly after leaving mine!'

Immediately Kate stiffened. 'You have no right to say that.'

'Do you think I don't know that?' Sean retaliated savagely. 'Don't you think I know that I have thrown away all my rights where you are concerned!'

'All your rights?' Horrified, Kate wondered what reckless surge of self-destruction had prompted such dangerous words, and spoken in such a soft, sexually challenging voice. And, as though that was not folly enough, she discovered that she had a sudden compulsion to let her gaze slide helplessly to Sean's mouth and then linger wantonly there, whilst her body reminded her hungrily of the pleasure he had once given it, how long it had been since…

'Kate, for God's sake, will you please stop looking at me like that?' Sean warned her harshly.

Mortified, she defended herself immediately, fibbing, 'I don't know what you mean!'

Instantly Sean took a step towards her, a look smouldering in the depths of his eyes that made a fierce thrill of dangerous excitement race through her.

'Liar! You know perfectly well what I mean.' Sean checked her thickly. 'You were looking at my mouth as though you couldn't wait to feel it against your own.'

What the hell was he doing? Sean challenged himself inwardly. His sole reason for having anything at all to do with Kate was to give her some much needed financial help, and that was all. Nothing else. Absolutely nothing else.

And yet within seconds of telling himself that, Sean could hear himself asking softly, 'Is that what you want, Kate? Because if it is…'

Just the sound of his voice was having a disturbingly erotic effect on her body—and on her senses. Defensively she closed her eyes, and then realised she had made a bad move as immediately she was swamped with mental images from the past.

Sean leaning over her in their bed, the morning sun on his bronzed skin, his eyes gleaming with sensual intent and knowledge between his narrowed eyelids. How quickly that cool look had grown hot and urgent when she had reached out to touch him, tugging teasingly on the fine hair covering his chest, before giving in to the erotic pleasure of sliding her fingers down the silky pathway which led over the hard flat plane of his belly to where the soft hair thickened.

Before she even realised what she was doing, never mind being able to stop herself, Kate felt her fingers stretching and curling, as though they could actually feel the strong, hard pulse of Sean's erection within their grip.

As soon as she realised what she was doing—and what she was feeling—Kate thrust her hands behind her back, guilty heat scorching her skin.

Angry both with herself for feeling the way she had and with Sean for being responsible for that feeling, she told him fiercely, 'No, it isn't.' She lied. 'Why should I want someone who did what you did? Someone who broke his marriage vows and took someone else to his bed? How could I want you, Scan?'

'Snap—that's exactly how I feel about you!' Sean stopped her passionately. 'You do realise, don't you, that I can throw the same accusations at you? How do you think it feels to discover that you didn't even wait a full month before jumping into bed with someone else? Why did you do that, Kate? Was it loneliness, or just spite?'

'I didn't do any such thing,' Kate denied shakily. His words had touched a wound in her heart that she had thought completely healed. But, as she had recently discovered, the scar tissue over it had been vulnerably fragile, and now the pain was agonisingly raw again.

Kate's face went white, but before she could say anything Sean had turned on his heel and was heading for the door.

'Don't come in to work tomorrow, and if Oliver isn't better by Monday let me know. And that's an order,' Sean instructed her grimly. 'I'll make arrangements to have your car brought here for you.'

## CHAPTER SIX

'WELL, Oliver might have escaped going down with the dreaded bug, but it doesn't look as though you've been quite so lucky,' Carol commented forthrightly as she studied Kate's wan face.

'I've had a bad night,' Kate admitted reluctantly.

Kate had met her friend as she walked Oliver to school, and now the two boys were walking together, leaving Kate to fall into step with Carol.

'My daddy can do anything,' Kate heard George boasting.

'Boys!' Carol laughed, shaking her head and exchanging a rueful look with Kate.

'Well, Sean can do everything in the whole world!'

Kate bit her lip as Oliver's voice rang out, miserably aware of the comprehensive and sympathetic look Carol was giving her.

'Sounds as though Sean is a big hit with Oliver,' she commented lightly, but Kate could guess what she was thinking. The griping pain in her stomach bit harder and she winced, causing Carol to exclaim with concern, 'You really aren't well, Kate, are you? You should be in bed! Look, why don't you go home and go back to bed? I'll take Oliver to school and collect him for you.'

'I can't. I've got to go to work,' Kate told her. 'I didn't go in on Friday because of Oliver. I can't take more time off.'

'Kate, you can't possibly go to work. You look dreadful,' Carol protested, adding worriedly, 'Look at you!

You're shivering, and it's nearly eighty degrees. This bug is really nasty if it gets a grip.'

'Thanks!' Kate said dryly, adding determinedly, 'Anyway, I'm fine.'

But she could see from her friend's face that Carol knew she was lying, and the truth was that she felt anything but fine.

Unlike Oliver, who had recovered from his upset tummy within a matter of hours, ever since she'd been sick the morning before she had steadily become more and more unwell. Her head felt as though it was being pounded with a sledgehammer, she had been sick on and off all night, and every bone in her body ached. She felt as if she was having flu and food poisoning all in one go.

Now the pain in her head increased, and when she closed her eyes against it a wave of nauseating dizziness hit her.

'No way are you going to work!' Carol's firm voice broke into her misery. 'How on earth are you planning to get there? You can't possibly drive. Go home, and as soon as I've dropped the boys off I'll call in and make sure you're okay.'

Another surge of nausea reinforced the truth of what Carol was saying, and, handing Oliver over to her, Kate hurriedly made her way back home. She was unable to tell which felt worse—the agonising pain in her head, which made her want to crawl into a dark place and with any luck die there, or the knowledge that unless she got home soon she was all too likely to be sick in public.

Half an hour later Carol returned from dropping the boys off. Kate was barely aware of her knocking and then entering through the back door.

'Thank goodness you've seen sense,' her friend exclaimed in relief, finding Kate safely tucked up in bed and adding with concern, 'I'd stay with you, but I promised I'd take my mother to hospital for her check-up today.'

'I'll be fine,' Kate assured her wanly. 'I just need to sleep off this headache, that's all.'

'Well, if you're sure…'

'I'm sure,' Kate insisted, only realising when Carol had gone that she ought to have asked her to telephone the office for her and explain what had happened.

Somehow just the thought of making the call herself was exhausting—and besides she needed to be sick again…

Sean frowned as his gaze flicked round Kate's empty office. Why hadn't she rung in? Was Oliver more seriously ill than anyone had realised?

It was the human resources department's responsibility to check up on why Kate hadn't reported in, not his, Sean reminded himself grimly. He was simply her employer now, and that was all.

A muscle twitched betrayingly in his jaw. Who the hell did he think he was deceiving?

He was supposed to be leaving here today, to return to headquarters for an important meeting, and he had not planned to come back until the following week.

If the woman in human resources was surprised that he should ask for Kate's home telephone number she was professional enough not to show it, Sean acknowledged.

In the privacy of his office Sean dialled the number, his frown deepening as it rang out unanswered.

* * *

Slipping in and out of a feverish half-sleep, Kate was vaguely aware of the telephone ringing, but she felt far too ill to get up and answer it.

Sean waited until he heard Kate's answering machine cut in before hanging up. Where on earth was she? Unwanted thoughts tormented his imagination. Kate sitting in a hospital waiting room whilst medical staff sped away with Oliver's vulnerable little-boy body... His feeling of anguish and anxiety, combined with a need to be there, surged through him and caught him off guard.

He would feel the same concern for any young child, Sean assured himself grittily. Just as he had been himself, Oliver was a fatherless child. He knew all too well how that felt. How it hurt.

A brief telephone call to Head Office was enough to cancel his meeting. How could he chair a meeting when Oliver might be ill?

He stuck it out for as long as he could, punctuating his anxiety with several more unsuccessful telephone calls, but midway through the afternoon he threw down the papers he was supposed to be studying and reached for his jacket.

When Sean reached Kate's house the open back door and the relief on two of the three anxious faces that turned towards him told its own story—or at least some of it.

'Sean!'

'Oh, thank goodness!'

As Oliver raced towards him Sean bent automatically to pick him up.

'My mummy is very sick,' Oliver said, causing Sean to grip Oliver tightly.

'Kate isn't at all well,' Carol explained quickly. 'In

fact when I came round with Oliver after school I was so worried I sent for the doctor.'

Sean looked at the tired-looking middle-aged man who was the third member of the trio.

'Kate appears to have contracted a particularly virulent strain of this current virus,' he explained wearily. 'She's dehydrated and very weak, and in no way able to look after herself at the moment—never mind her child. She needs someone here to make sure she drinks plenty of fluids and generally look after her.'

He was looking meaningfully at Carol, who bit her lip and told him uncomfortably, 'Normally I would have been only too happy to have Oliver to stay, but—'

'That won't be necessary,' Sean announced firmly, breaking into the conversation. 'I'll stay with Kate and look after her and Oliver. I'm her ex-husband,' he explained tersely, when he saw the doctor beginning to frown.

'I should warn you that she's only semi-conscious,' the doctor told him sharply, after Carol had left to go back to her own family. 'And slightly delirious and confused in fact,' he added. 'But that will pass. She's got a high fever, combined with stomach cramps. I have given her some medication which should start to make her feel better within the next twelve hours, although it will be considerably longer than that before she starts to recover properly and—'

'Why the hell aren't you admitting her to hospital?' Sean demanded angrily.

'For several reasons,' the doctor answered. 'One, I doubt very much that I could get her a bed. Two, she has a child, who will no doubt be distressed by such an action. And three, whilst she's very unwell, her condition isn't acute. I appreciate that looking after her isn't going to be easy. If you're having second thoughts then perhaps you could let me know now, because I shall have to organise some kind of temporary foster care for the child and a district nurse to call round when she can to check on my patient.'

'Foster care! Oliver doesn't need foster care and Kate doesn't need the district nurse—they've got me,' Sean announced protectively.

The doctor tried not to show his relief. This virus was stretching local medical resources beyond their limits.

'Very well. Now, this is what you will have to do…'

Sean listened grimly as the doctor gave him his instructions.

Oliver was still nestled sleepily in his arms, and after the doctor had gone Oliver looked up into Sean's face and demanded anxiously, 'When is my mummy going to get better?'

'Soon,' Sean assured him calmly, but inwardly he was feeling very far from calm.

Ten minutes later, as he stood beside the bed looking down into Kate's pale face whilst she lay frighteningly still, he felt even less so. Her left hand lay limply on top of the duvet, her fingers ringless and her nails free of polish. She had beautiful hands and fragile, delicate wrists, he reflected sombrely. They had been one the first things about her he had noticed. Now, if anything, her wrist looked even narrower than he remembered.

Suddenly she made a restless movement and turned her hand over. He could see the blueness of her veins through the fine skin. Beads of sweat burst out on her forehead and she moaned suddenly, shivering violently, her eyes opening and then widening in confusion and bewilderment as she saw him.

'It's all right, Kate,' Sean reassured her as she looked vaguely up at him. But even as he was trying to reassure her Sean knew that he could not reassure himself. He could feel the heavy, agonised thud of his heartbeat.

'My head hurts,' Kate told him plaintively.

'Why don't you sit up and drink some of this water, take these tablets the doctor has left for you?' Sean suggested gently. 'They should bring your temperature down and help you to feel better.'

Obediently she tried to do as he suggested, but Sean could see that even the small effort of trying to sit up was too much for her.

Without giving her the chance to protest, he sat down on the bed and put his arm round her, supporting her as he plumped up the pillows.

She was wearing some kind of cotton nightshirt, which was soaked with sweat and damp, and as he supported her she started to shiver so violently that her teeth chattered together.

It made Sean's own throat hurt to see the difficulty she had swallowing even a few sips of water.

'My throat hurts so much,' she whispered to him as she pushed the glass away. 'Everything hurts.'

Automatically Sean placed his hand against her forehead.

'That feels good,' she told him quietly. 'Cool.'

Sean had to swallow back the feelings both her words and the burning hot feel of her skin had aroused.

'I feel so hot,' she complained fretfully.

'You've got a bad virus,' Sean told her.

'I don't want to keep you away from work, Sean. Not with the Anderson contract to get finished.'

Her eyes were closing as he lowered her back against the pillows, and Sean watched her with a frown. The

Anderson contract she had referred to was one he had worked on in the early days of their marriage.

'Slightly delirious.' The doctor had warned him. And she was wringing wet, burning up and shivering at the same time.

She had been his wife, his lover, and her body held no secrets from him. How could it when she had given herself so freely to him, when he had been the one to help her to explore and discover the power of its female sexuality? Even so he could feel his muscles clenching as he worked to remove her fever-sodden nightshirt, blessing the fact that it fastened down the front with buttons. Or was it a blessing? Instead of removing it quickly he was having to fight against the savage stab of arousal he felt when he exposed the pale curves of her breasts, to force himself to ignore the sensuality of her naked body and to focus on her illness instead.

Reluctant to search through her drawers for a clean nightshirt, after he had sponged down her fever-soaked body he wrapped her in a towel instead, answering the disjointed questions she asked when she woke up briefly.

By the time he was satisfied that she was both dry and warm, and was finally able to cover her with the duvet, his hands were shaking.

'Sean?'

He froze as he realised she had woken up again. 'Yes?' he replied.

'I love you so much,' she told him simply, smiling sweetly at him before she closed her eyes and drifted back to sleep.

There was, Sean discovered, a dangerous pain inside his chest, and the backs of his eyes were burning, as though they had been soaked with limewash.

* * *

It was two o'clock in the morning and Sean was exhausted. Kate's temperature seemed to have dropped a little, much to his relief. And Oliver was fast asleep in his own bed, unaware of the sharp pangs of emotion Sean had felt when Oliver had solemnly explained to him his bedtime routine.

Suppressing a yawn, Sean pushed his hand through his hair. Kate was asleep but he was reluctant to leave her.

He went into the bathroom and had a shower. It had been a long day. His eyes felt gritty and tired. He looked at the empty half of the bed. It wasn't going to hurt anyone if he just lay down and snatched a few minutes' sleep, was it?

Kate could feel the pain of her anguished despair. A bleak, searing sense of loss engulfed her, lacerated by panic and agonising disbelief. In her jumbled fever-induced dream she ran on leaden legs from room to room of a shadowed empty house, frantically searching for Sean whilst the icy-cold tentacles of her fear took hold of her heart.

Sean had left her and she couldn't bear the pain of losing him. She couldn't endure the thought of living without him. She felt bereft, abandoned, and totally alone.

The pain of her dream was unbearable, and she fought to escape from it, dragging herself frantically through the layers of sleep, crying out Sean's name as she did so.

The moment he heard Kate cry out, Sean was awake.

'Sean?'

He could hear the panic in her voice as she repeated

his name, and even in the semi-darkness he could see how her body was shaking.

'Kate, it's all right,' he tried to reassure her, and he placed his hand on her arm and leaned over her.

Kate could feel herself shaking with the intensity of the emotions flooding through her, piercing her muddled confusion. When she managed to force her eyes open she exhaled in relief. She could see Sean's familiar outline in the bed! Sean was here. He had not left her! She had just been having a bad dream!

But, despite her relief, somewhere on the edge of her consciousness something was niggling at her—something she did not want to recognise. Defensively she pushed it away, escaping instead into the comforting security of Sean's presence. But she needed more than just his presence to banish the dark shadows of the dream, she recognised.

Instinctively she moved towards him, wanting, needing to be closer to him. Although her brain felt muddled, and somehow not fully functioning, her senses were sharply acute and her whole body shuddered as she breathed in his warm, musky scent. She could feel the familiar arousal taking over her body.

She wanted Sean to hold her.

'Hold me close, Sean,' she begged huskily, shivering as she told him in a low, unsteady voice, 'I was dreaming that you weren't here… And everything seems so muddled. I can't seem to think straight…'

'You've had a bad virus and a high fever,' Sean told her quietly, deliberately using the past tense so that he didn't frighten her.

'I think I must have been suffering from delusions.' Kate tried to laugh, but her smile disappeared as her whole body shuddered violently. 'It was so frightening,

Sean,' she whispered. 'I dreamt that I was in a house looking for you but you weren't there.'

Emotional tears filled her eyes and Sean listened helplessly. Fever burned in her face and glazed her eyes. She made a small movement towards him and Sean began to draw back. But it was too late. Kate was already nestling trustingly into him.

Sombrely Sean looked down at her. His throat felt tight and he was acutely conscious that this should not be happening. Right now his role was that of nurse and guardian—but how could he explain that to her in her present confused and feverish condition? Would she even understand what he was trying to say? Somehow Sean doubted it. And, as though to confirm his thoughts, he felt her move, saw that his slight hesitation had made her focus on him, her anxious gaze searching his face.

'Sean?' she questioned as she reached out and curled her fingers onto the polished skin of his shoulder.

And then, before he could stop her, she moved closer to him and pressed her face against his chest.

Eagerly Kate snuggled closer to the security of Sean's body. Just breathing in the familiar scent of him was immediately reassuring and calming. Calming? When had anything to do with being close to Sean had a calming effect on her? Kate smiled inwardly at herself. Calm was certainly not the way she was feeling right now, with her heart hammering and her body feeling so ridiculously weak. Weak, maybe, but also acutely and erotically aware of Sean. And her physical longing was heightened by the intensity of her aching, emotional need to be close to him.

It was as though her dream had left her with a vulnerability that only Sean's intimate closeness could repair, Kate acknowledged vaguely. Dismissing her thoughts, she nuzzled into the warmth of his chest, tasting it with absorbed delight. And then, whilst Sean was still grappling with his own shock, she moved her head and placed her lips against his flesh, openly luxuriating in the pleasure of slowly and languorously caressing him.

Sean could feel the shallow, rapid race of his heartbeat as he tensed his body against its immediate reaction to her. He had never for one minute imagined, and certainly not intended anything like this should happen.

But now that it had…

Now that it had he was having to battle against the reality of the situation, against the achingly sensual pleasure of Kate half lying over him. There was no way he could allow himself to even acknowledge what it did to him, having the softness of her lips delicately brushing his skin.

If he didn't put an end to what was happening, and soon, he would be in danger of racing out of control and down a road he had no right to travel. A road which Kate in full health would refuse to allow him to travel.

Determinedly Sean reached out and closed his hands around her upper arms, intending to lift her away from his body and place her back on her own half of the bed. But the minute he tried to move her she moaned and clung to him.

It was more than his self-control could bear.

Sean swallowed hard. He had to put a stop to this.

'Kate—'

'Mmm…' Kate exhaled on an ecstatic sigh as she pressed a small kiss to the corner of Sean's mouth. Helplessly he returned it—with interest—whilst inside him a savagely bitter voice reminded him condemningly that Kate was sick, that she did not really know what was happening, and that just because she was kissing him back, and trying to touch him, it did not mean that he should let her.

It took all the strength he had to lift his mouth from the sweetness of her, and when he did she looked up at him in confused bewilderment.

He had to put a stop to this, and he had to do it now, Sean told himself fiercely.

But the look in Kate's eyes made him want to take her in his arms and hold her there until it disappeared.

The duvet had slipped away to reveal the curves of her breasts, palely silvered by the moonlight streaming in through the window, in contrast to the sensually darkened areolae from which her nipples rose in stiffly erect peaks.

Dizzily Kate watched with open sensual pleasure as she saw Sean's gaze fasten helplessly on her exposed breasts. But she knew that she wanted to feel more than his hot gaze touching her. A fierce shudder gripped her, making her gasp and exhale.

And as he watched her, and recognised what she was feeling, somehow, without him knowing how it had happened, Sean started to lower his mouth towards her lips.

Eagerly Kate offered herself up for Sean's possession, her hands reaching out with surprising strength to draw him to her waiting body. A wild shudder contorted her as she parted her lips for the driving pressure of his tongue, her own mating with it.

Beneath his hands Sean could feel the familiarity of her—the longed-for and long-loved familiarity of her—and it was more than his self-control could stand. He hadn't meant for his hand to touch her breast, to slowly caress its fullness as it swelled sweetly into his hand, and he certainly hadn't intended to allow his fingers to stroke softly against her thigh as she trembled beneath his touch. Dear heaven, he should not be permitting this, Sean admitted helplessly. He should be putting in place the barriers between them that Kate could not. He should be stopping what was happening, not feeling that he would die if he did not hold her and love her.

His need was overruling his conscience and his self-control. The tight, swollen feel of the nipple pressing into his hand, the feel of Kate's mouth against his skin, the knowledge that he had only to move his hand and place it between her open thighs to feel the familiar pleasure of her sweet, wet warmth, was obliterating everything but his overpowering need for her.

He moved her body and cupped her face, kissing her until she was moaning longingly beneath his mouth, her hands seeking his hard arousal as hungrily as his were seeking the swollen wetness of hers.

He kissed her breasts, slowly and then far more fiercely, making her shudder with desire as she felt the rough sensual lapping of his tongue against the sensitivity of her nipples, then cry out in primitive female pleasure when his mouth closed over one swollen peak.

Her own hand pressed over the hand he had placed between her thighs, holding it there as his fingers caressed her receptive flesh.

Sean felt that his actions were not premeditated so much as preordained. What was happening between them just seemed so natural, so right—and so very, very much what their bodies wanted. So much so, in fact, that for a few seconds he allowed himself to suspend reality and give in to his love.

Almost as soon as he touched her intimately Sean heard Kate cry out as her body quickened to his touch. Her hands clamped around his arm as though seeking and needing reassurance—and the small, almost startled cry ended as the contractions of her orgasm began.

'Sean,' Kate whispered dreamily, with appreciative pleasure, lifting her hand to touch his face, but she was asleep before she could finish doing so.

Numbly Sean waited until he was sure that Kate was deeply asleep before moving away from her. He could not comprehend how he had allowed things to get so out of hand, why he had not somehow stopped. Not so much Kate, but more importantly himself. Why and how had he allowed his feelings to become so out of control that he had given in to them? A stab of revulsion against himself hit him like a sledgehammer-blow to his heart.

Deep down inside Sean, despite the trauma of his childhood, was a core of pure old-fashioned male protectiveness that was an essential part of how he regarded himself. As a man who would protect the woman he loved—from everything and everyone, even including himself, if and when necessary. Wasn't that, after all, why he had divorced Kate in the first place? So that she should be free to have with another man the children he knew he could not give her.

That element of his personality was of vital importance to him; it underpinned his sense of who he was and his pride in himself. But how could he be proud of himself now? As his anger against himself grew Sean paced the floor of Kate's room, refusing to allow himself to escape from his own contempt.

A sound from the bed—a whimper and then a small burst of unintelligible words—caused him to freeze, and then go to Kate's side.

It was obvious that the fever was mounting again, and when he woke her to give her the medication the doctor had left, and to make sure she drank some water, the blank, unseeing look she gave him made Sean suspect that she didn't even realise who he was…

She would hate knowing that she had clung to him and begged him to love her, he recognised grimly. Although he doubted that in her feverish state she would remember what had happened. She would certainly not *want* to remember it; he knew that.

But when he laid her down again, and sponged her hot skin, Sean acknowledged that he would remember it, that he would store the memory deep inside himself, where he had already stored so many memories of her.

Bleakly he looked away from her. The pain inside him that never went away was tearing at his gut. Just being here in this small house intensified it almost beyond bearing. Within this house were the woman he loved, always would love, and the child he would give his life to have been able to give her. Kate had no idea what she did to him when she tried to insist that Oliver was his son.

Kate could feel the warmth of sunlight on her closed eyelids. Weakly she struggled to understand the feeling of panic that the warmth engendered, her body stiffening as the knowledge hit her that the sunlight only shone through her bedroom window early in the afternoon.

As she opened her eyes she tried to sit up in her bed, only to collapse against her pillows as her virus-weakened body refused to support her. Shock and panic spiked through her, multiplied by fear as she realised how quiet the house was.

Where was Oliver, and why was she here in bed? She had to get up and find her son. Shakily she pushed back the bedclothes, frowning in alarmed bewilderment as she looked down at the unfamiliar sea-green fine cotton nightgown she was wearing, its hem and bodice lavishly trimmed with expensive lace.

Instinctively she touched the fabric. Once, long ago, she had owned such things—not that she had ever worn them very much. Her expression changed. Sean had always preferred them to sleep skin to skin, and so had she. A tiny shudder gripped her body as a vague, unsettling memory—confusing misty images of Sean and her as lovers—stirred inside her head like ripples on water. And just as elusive to grasp. But she had an urgent and anxious feeling that she had to grasp it.

Her heart was hammering against her ribs; she felt oddly disorientated—light-headed, almost. She put her feet on the floor and stood up, shocked to discover that her legs could barely support her and that she had to cling to the side of the bed.

Whilst she was struggling to keep her balance the bedroom door opened, but her initial relief was quickly swamped by angry panic when she saw Sean coming towards her. Immediately she backed up towards the bed. Sean stood still.

Shockingly surreal and unwanted mental flashbacks were tormenting her. Disjointed but frighteningly potent memories of Sean and herself as lovers, of herself begging Sean to make love to her.

Nausea and pain tore at her in equal measures. She could hardly bring herself to look at him. Her head was pounding, and with every second that passed she felt weaker.

'Where's Oliver?' she demanded anxiously. 'And what are you doing here?'

'Oliver's at nursery, and I'm here because both you and he needed someone here to look after you.'

'To look after me? You've been looking after me?'

Try as she might, Kate couldn't keep the near hysterical anguish out of her voice. 'Why you?'

'Why not me? I was here, and I am your ex-husband.' He gave a small dismissive shrug.

'My ex-husband?'

'There was no one else, Kate.' Sean stopped her almost gently. 'Your friend Carol wanted to help, but she has a husband and a child of her own. I did wonder at one stage if perhaps hospital...'

'Hospital?' Kate could feel the terrifyingly heavy thud of her heart.

'The virus you've had hit you very hard,' Sean told her patiently, adding, 'Look, why don't you get back into bed—?' As he spoke he came towards her.

'No! Don't touch me,' Kate protested in panic when he looked as if he were about to pick her up.

The way he was looking at her made her flush painfully, her skin burning. Just having him stand so close to her was activating all kinds of disturbing memories. It wasn't just some feverish act of her imagination that was responsible, Kate acknowledged miserably. The memories were there because it had happened. She had said and done all those things she was being forced to remember.

Helplessly she waited for Sean to mock and taunt her with the words she could hear ringing so clearly inside her own head, to remind her that she had already begged him to do far more than merely touch her. Instead he said nothing, simply bent down to pick her up and placed her firmly back in the bed.

'You're still very weak—' he told her, and then broke off as the doorbell rang. 'That will be the doctor. I'll go down and let him in.'

As soon as he had gone Kate lifted her hand to her

forehead and pressed her skin tightly as she tried to force herself to remember exactly what had happened. Humiliatingly, all her body could and would remember was the pleasure Sean had given it, whilst inside her head she could hear the ringing echo of her own passionate pleas for his possession.

The bedroom door reopened and Sean ushered in the doctor, whose face was full of concern.

'So, Kate, you are back with us. Good! Your husband has obviously done an excellent job of looking after you.'

Her husband! Kate wanted to remind the doctor that Sean was her ex-husband, but somehow it was too much of an effort. The frightening realisation of just how physically weak she felt was just beginning to hit her.

'You are over the worst now, but that does not mean you are better. You are very far from better,' the doctor told her emphatically.

'So when will I be better?' Kate demanded, with a show of energy she was far from feeling. A little uncomfortably she saw that the doctor was looking at her as though he knew perfectly well how she was really feeling.

'Well, if you do as you are told, and don't try to rush things, I would say that you will be fully back to normal in three weeks or so.'

'Three weeks!' Kate struggled to sit up as she stared at him in shock. 'But, no! That's impossible!' she started to tell him frantically. 'I need to find a new job! I have to go back to work. I've just had a bit of a virus, that's all—it can't possibly take three weeks for me to get better!'

'You've had a very serious strain of the virus, and without wanting to frighten you…' the doctor paused.

'It is fortunate that you have such a naturally strong constitution,' he told her 'And as for you going back to work…' He shook his head. 'No, you cannot do that.'

'Nor will she be doing that, Doctor.' Sean joined the conversation grimly, giving Kate a warning look as he added smoothly, 'I know that no employer would allow her to work anyway, until she has been given a clean bill of health.'

Kate felt distraught, but she had to satisfy herself with giving Sean a seethingly furious look as he escorted the doctor to the door.

When he came back, she told him determinedly, 'I can't not work for three weeks! I would have found a new job by now if I hadn't been ill,' she added fretfully.

When Sean remained silent she reminded him angrily, 'I have to work. I have a child to support and a mortgage to pay.'

'We'll talk about this later,' Sean said in a clipped voice. 'It's time for me to go and collect Oliver from nursery.'

Kate wanted to argue, but her head was pounding and all she could do was watch him leave with helpless fury.

It just wasn't possible that it would take three weeks before she was back to normal! She was sure the doctor was exaggerating her weakness—no doubt prompted and aided by Sean, she decided, scowling. And she was going to prove it!

The moment she heard Sean leave she thrust back the bedcovers, refusing to acknowledge that even that action left her arms aching. She was in her twenties, for heaven's sake, not in her nineties, she reminded herself determinedly, and she ignored her dizziness.

Placing her feet firmly on the floor, she stood up, and immediately had to make a wild grab for the bed as her legs refused to support her properly. Okay, she was feeling a little bit weak—but that was because she hadn't been doing anything, because she had been lying in bed and not using her muscles.

Kate could feel her face starting to burn as she was forced to remember just what she had done in bed. And as she clung unsteadily to the bed other vague images wove themselves in and out of her memory: strong arms lifting and holding her, supporting her whilst she drank, careful hands soothing her hot and hurting skin, the presence of a shadowy but oh-so-comforting figure doing for her everything that needed to be done, even anticipating her every need.

Shakily Kate wondered for just how long the fever had consumed her. She touched her hair; it felt clean and soft. She had an immediate and shocking image of being held beneath the shower, whilst blissfully cleansing water cascaded over her sticky and uncomfortable body.

Sean had done all those things for her. Sean had cared for her as though…as though… As though they were still a couple—a pair bonded together by mutual love and commitment. As though he still loved her!

But he had abandoned her for someone else, she reminded herself fiercely as she forced her weak aching legs to move. He had given the love she had thought exclusively hers to another woman. No matter what her deepest and most secret feelings, she must not allow herself to forget that betrayal.

Her deepest and most secret feelings? A recognition she did not want to acknowledge tightened its hurting grasp around her heart. Gritting her teeth, she took three steps, and then gasped out loud with shock as her legs refused to support her any longer and she sank awkwardly to the floor.

Ten minutes later she was safely back in bed—her bones, never mind her flesh, feeling as though they had been pummelled and bruised, every bit of her filled with an aching, nagging pain she couldn't ignore.

Kate had never really been physically ill, and the only real physical pain she had had to endure was when she had given birth to Oliver—and anyway, that had been different.

This unfamiliar aching weakness was alien to her, and very frightening. She loathed the thought of being dependent on anyone, no matter who it might be, and that it should be Sean brought a whole raft of emotional complications she just did not feel able to cope with. But she was going to have to cope with them. Because, as she had just proved to herself, the doctor had been quite correct—she was far too weak to even look after herself, never mind care properly for Oliver, or find a new job!

Angry tears burned the backs of her eyes, followed by a feeling of panicky fear. How was she going to manage? How would she support them both? It seemed so unfair that after all the hard work she had done this should happen—now when she had finally begun to allow herself to hope that her plans for their financial security would be successful. Hastily she blinked the tears away as she heard the door open, followed by the sound of Oliver's excited voice.

The sight of him bursting into her room and running towards her, followed by Sean, immediately lifted her spirits—although she frowned a little to see that he was wearing obviously new clothes she didn't recognise.

As though he could guess what she was thinking, Sean

explained carelessly, 'I couldn't get the washing dry because of the rain, so I bought some new stuff.'

Oliver had reached the bed and was scrambling onto it. As she reached down to help him Kate saw the labels on the new clothes and her mouth compressed, her panic returning. Expensive designer labels! How on earth was she going to repay Sean for them? She had only ever been able to afford to buy Oliver good second-hand clothes, and sometimes new things from chain stores.

'Mummy, you're properly awake at last!' Oliver beamed as he kissed her enthusiastically. 'Look what I painted for you!' he said, triumphantly showing her the brightly painted paper he was holding.

'It's me and you and Sean, and Sean's house where we're all going to live.' Immediately Kate went still, keeping her arm around her son whilst she looked accusingly at Sean. Her heart was pounding so heavily that it hurt.

'What—?' she began fiercely, but Sean was already lifting Oliver off the bed.

'Come on,' he was saying to Oliver. 'Let's go downstairs and make Mummy some tea. We'll talk later,' he added quietly to Kate.

'Yes, and then I'll read you a story, Mummy,' Oliver told her happily. 'We've read you a story every night—haven't we, Sean? But you weren't properly awake. Having lots of sleep made you get better, though,' he informed Kate importantly. With a graveness that tore at her heart, Oliver continued, 'You have to have lots of water to drink, doesn't she, Sean?'

'Lots of water, and now some proper food,' Sean agreed calmly.

Kate could feel her eyes smarting with emotional tears as Sean disappeared with Oliver.

She had been miserably worried about her illness affecting Oliver emotionally, but now it was plain to her that she had worried unnecessarily. Because Oliver had had Sean. Because Oliver had had his father.

A huge groundswell of emotional pain began deep down inside her. How could Sean behave as he was doing with Oliver and yet at the same time so completely reject the fact that Oliver was his son? And as for Oliver's innocent remark about them going to live with Sean!

Tiredness began to swamp her, overwhelming her angry attempts to fight it off and remain awake.

When Sean walked into the bedroom five minutes later she was fast asleep. Putting down the tray holding the pot of tea he had brewed for her, and the light omelette he had just made, Sean went over to look at her, frowning deeply as he did so. The previous day the doctor had told him that he believed she was over the worst, and today, with her return to full consciousness, Sean had seen that for himself.

He was reluctant to wake her up, but he knew that she needed to start eating again in order to build up her strength.

Going over to her, he reached out to touch her, and then hesitated. The strap of the nightdress he had bought her when he had been forced to go out and buy food and extra clothes for Oliver had slipped down over her exposed shoulder.

Without thinking, his actions still on the automatic pilot of having looked after her, he curled his fingers around the strap and started to tug it back up.

Kate woke up immediately, her whole body tensing as she saw Sean leaning over her.

The sight of the afternoon sunshine falling against his

skin made her stifle a small sound deep in her throat. She had never admitted it to him, but she could still remember how all those years ago, when they had first met, she had deliberately walked past the building site where he was working, unable to stop her avid gaze feeding hungrily on the sight of his naked torso, pin-pricks of dangerous excitement prickling all over her body. Just as they were doing now, Kate realised, as the emotions she was fighting to hold in check swept through her.

She must not allow herself to react to him like this, she told herself fiercely. She must not weaken and let him touch her emotions. She must not forget now much he had hurt her and, much more importantly, how much he could still hurt Oliver.

Thinking of her son gave her the strength to drag her gaze from Sean's and look pointedly at where his hand still rested on her shoulder.

'You must let me know how much you have spent on mine and Oliver's behalf,' she told him stiffly. She knew just from the feel of the fabric against her skin that the nightdress would have cost far more than she would ever have paid—and far more than she could possibly afford. But no way was she going to be beholden to him, even though she felt sick at the thought of having to waste her small precious savings on such unnecessary luxuries.

'There are several things we need to discuss,' Sean told her equably. 'But first you must have something to eat.'

Rebelliously Kate looked at him, the words 'I'm not hungry' dying on her lips as he added gently, 'Doctor's orders, Kate, and if necessary I can assure you I am perfectly willing to feed you myself.'

'That won't be necessary.'

'Good.'

Unable to contain herself any longer, she burst out, 'I can't be off work for three weeks.'

'You can't *not* be,' he corrected her curtly. 'And personally I don't think that your doctor is going to change his mind and allow you to return to work sooner. I take it that you haven't found another job as yet?'

Kate's mouth compressed whilst she contemplated lying to him, but then she was forced to admit that she was unlikely to get away with doing so. 'No,' she answered tersely. 'But I intend to spend the time I have to have off work looking for one.'

'On the contrary,' Sean told her firmly. 'What you are going to be spending the next three weeks doing is recuperating, as I am sure your doctor will inform you. But if you don't believe me you can check with him yourself. He'll be coming back to see you tomorrow, to make sure you're well enough to travel to…' He paused, and then continued coolly, 'To my home.'

'What?' Kate went hot and then cold with shock and disbelief. 'Oh, no. No way!' Kate shook her head violently. 'No way am I ever, *ever* going to live with you again, Sean…'

'Oliver is already looking forward to it,' he said blandly.

Kate felt as though she had been kicked in the stomach. 'You had no right to say anything to Oliver. Nor to use him to—'

'To what?' Sean challenged her. 'Right now you need someone to look after you—someone to look after you both. Physically and financially,' he emphasised unkindly.

'You don't know anything about my financial situation,' Kate denied hotly. 'And you have no right—'

'I know that on the salary you are being paid, given the outgoings you must have, you will have to budget carefully.' He gave a small shrug to conceal from her what he was really feeling. 'Logically it seems unlikely that you have a financial cushion to fall back on if, for instance, you are unable to work. As is the case now!'

Kate could feel a dangerous prickle in her throat as her emotions reacted to his extremely accurate assessment of her situation.

'I may not have your wealth, Sean, but I don't need your charity, or—' she began, only to be cut short as Sean interrupted her.

'Not for yourself, maybe, Kate. But you do need it for Oliver's sake—and don't bother trying to deny it!' He gave another dismissive shrug and turned slightly away from her so that she couldn't read his expression.

Helplessly Kate acknowledged that what Sean had said to her was true. For Oliver's sake she had no option other than to give in and agree to what Sean was suggesting.

Besides, wasn't there somewhere deep inside her still a foolish little shoot of hope that, given time and the opportunity to be with Oliver, Sean would somehow recognise and accept that Ollie was his child? And a part of her wanted that desperately—not for her own sake, but for their son's.

'The only person you have is me!' Sean told her abruptly. 'Unless, of course, you want to get in touch with Oliver's father,' he added harshly, shattering her fragile fantasy.

Kate felt sick with rage and pain. She wanted to scream at him that she did not need anyone, and that if she did need someone she would die before she let that someone be him.

'Carol will help me,' she began sharply, but Sean immediately shook his head.

'She has her own family to look after; you know that! And besides—'

'Besides what?' she demanded angrily.

'Besides, I don't think it would be in Oliver's best interests.'

For a few seconds Kate was rendered speechless with disbelief. When she did find her voice she could hear it trembling with the intensity of her rage.

'You don't think—! Since when have you concerned yourself with Oliver's best interests? Or don't you think it would be in Oliver's "best interests",' she mimicked, 'to be acknowledged and loved by his father?'

'Oh, for God's sake.'

Kate flinched as she heard the savagery in his voice.

'Regardless of who Oliver's father is, you are his mother and Oliver should be near you. If Carol were to look after you both that would necessitate her having Oliver spending a great deal of time at her house, away from you. I'm not denying that she would do her best for both of you, but...'

Kate closed her eyes. She knew exactly what Sean was saying, and what he was not saying—and, even worse, she knew that he was right.

'So who are you proposing will look after us?' she asked defeatedly.

'Me.'

Kate lifted her head and stared at him. 'You? No... That's not possible!'

'On the contrary, as I think I have proved these last few days, it is perfectly possible.'

'But you have to work. You've got your business to run,' Kate reminded him wildly.

'I can run my business from home,' Sean answered laconically. 'And it seems to me that I can look after you and Oliver and work much more easily in a house with more than two bedrooms. At least that way I'll have my own bed to sleep in.'

His own bed!

Kate could feel her anger giving way to panic. This was definitely not a line of conversation she wanted to pursue.

'So where is this house with more than two bedrooms?' she forced herself to demand. 'Oliver is very happy at nursery, and I don't want him upset.'

'Oliver won't be upset. It's only for a short while, and he needs to get used to change as he'll soon be leaving nursery anyway, to start school.' He started to frown. 'Your nearest infant school is nearly ten miles away...'

'I know that,' Kate snapped at him. Of course she knew it! Hadn't she been worrying herself sick for the last year about the fact that the village was too small to have its own school?

'Oliver has got used to having me around,' Sean said abruptly as he walked away from the bed and stood with his back to her, looking out of the window. 'It seems unfair and definitely not in his best interests to subject him to further changes. He's naturally been very upset by your illness, but he's looking forward to the three of us being together.'

The three of us!

A fierce pang of sharp pain stabbed at Kate's heart. How could she deny her son the opportunity to be with his father?

# CHAPTER SEVEN

'Now, don't worry about the cottage. I'll keep an eye on it whilst you're away, and it will be here waiting for you when you come back,' Carol assured Kate comfortingly as she bustled around Kate's bedroom, packing her clothes in the suitcases Sean had provided. 'That is if you are coming back,' she added slyly, giving Kate a questioning look. 'Sean's made no bones about telling everyone that the two of you were married.'

Carol's teasing expression changed to one of anxious concern as she saw the tears filling Kate's eyes. 'Oh, Kate, I'm so sorry,' she apologised.

'It's all right,' Kate assured her. 'I suppose feeling emotionally weak is just another manifestation of this wretched virus. Why has this had to happen to me? All I want is for the next three weeks to be over and for me to be back on my feet,' she told her friend fiercely.

'Mmm. Well, Oliver is certainly enjoying having Sean in his life,' Carol said with gentle warning. 'On the way to school this morning I overheard him trying to convince Sean that a puppy was an essential addition to his life.'

Kate groaned. 'He's been on about having a dog ever since he saw the puppies at the farm last year. I'd love to get him one, but it's just not possible with me working.'

'Heavens, I think Sean's bought you and Oliver enough clothes to last twelve months, never mind three weeks.' Carol laughed, ruefully. 'He'll be back soon, and

I know he wants to get off as soon as he can. Where is this house you're going to be staying, by the way?' she asked Kate conversationally, and she ruthlessly squashed the last of the new clothes Sean had insisted on buying for Kate and Oliver into the new cases, whilst Kate looked on unhappily.

'I don't know,' she admitted, for the moment more concerned about her irritation with Sean for bringing yet more new clothes that morning than the location of his home.

'Oliver and I aren't charity cases, you know,' she had thrown bitingly at him when he had arrived back from his shopping spree. 'We don't need you to buy clothes for us, Sean.'

'Oliver is outgrowing virtually everything he has,' Sean had replied quietly. 'And, so far as I can tell, your own clothes—'

'Are my own concern,' Kate had snapped viciously.

Sean hadn't made any further response, but Kate had seen the warning grimness of his mouth as he listened to her churlish outburst.

'Okay, that's the car packed.'

Kate forced a smile for Carol and her husband, Tom, who had come round to see them off. Her smile turned to an anxious frown as Oliver and George came rushing towards them, and Oliver missed a step and fell.

Tom was standing closest to him and automatically bent down to pick him up, smiling reassuringly at him as Oliver's bottom lip thrust out and began to wobble.

'I'll take him!'

Kate's head swivelled round in Sean's direction when she heard the curtness in his voice, and she saw the immediate and determined way in which he went to take

Oliver from the other man. When he held Oliver there was a look in his eyes that made Kate's heart turn over. Sean had resented the fact that Tom had gone to Oliver's rescue!

The scuffed knee and bruised pride attended to, Sean put Oliver down whilst he helped Kate to the car. She could walk a few yards now, but she had to admit that it was easier to lean on Sean than to insist on walking by herself. There was surely no real need, though, for Sean to fasten her seat belt for her?

In the enclosed space of the car she was acutely conscious of the scent of his skin, and of the way the dark bristles of his beard were already roughening his jaw. If she leaned forward only just a little she would be able to press her lips to his skin. Her heart turned over and she gazed at him whilst he was absorbed in his task of making her comfortable. The dark thick fans of his eyelashes cast shadows over his skin, making him look unfairly vulnerable. His concentration on his task reminded her poignantly of Oliver whenever he was engrossed in something.

A small sound bubbled in her throat and Sean turned to look at her. At her and into her. His gaze fastened on her eyes and then dropped with merciless swiftness to her mouth. Kate felt her lips parting as though he had willed them to do so. A small, fine shudder ran through her, and she knew exactly why Sean was no longer looking at her or through her, but at her breasts. She could feel the tight betraying stiffness of her nipples as they responded to her sudden arousal.

'When are we going?'

Oliver's impatient demand brought Kate swiftly back to reality.

'We are going right now,' Sean answered him, standing up and closing the passenger door.

Not even the comfort of Sean's luxurious saloon could completely prevent her body from aching, and by the time they had been travelling for three hours all Kate wanted to do was to be able to lie down and go to sleep, but when Sean asked her if she was all right she nodded, refusing to admit how very uncomfortable and exhausted she felt.

'I'm fine,' she insisted doggedly, refusing to look at him even though she knew he had turned his head to look at her.

'There's bound to be a hotel somewhere round here,' was Sean's undeceived and clipped response. 'We can stop there and you can rest.'

'No,' Kate protested. Hotels, like the new clothes Sean had bought for them, cost money—and she was determined that somehow she was going to repay him every penny he had spent on them.

She hadn't realised that Sean's house was going to be so far away, but her pride would not allow her to ask him exactly where it was or how long it would take them to get there.

Oliver, though, had no such inhibitions, and demanded, 'Are we nearly there yet?'

'Almost,' Sean assured him, without turning his head, and Kate knew that he was smiling because she could hear the smile in his voice.

A wave of tiredness swamped her and she started to slip in her seat, unaware of the anxious look Sean was giving her.

'Not much further now,' she heard him saying quietly.

'Just another couple of junctions on the motorway and then we'll be turning off. We can stop then, and—'

'I've already told you that I don't want to stop,' Kate burst out irritably. 'I never even wanted to go to this wretched house of yours in the first place!' she reminded him bitterly.

As she struggled to make herself comfortable she intercepted the wholly male look her son and his father were exchanging. Anger and anguish tore at her in equal measures—because these two males who shared one another's blood had bonded against her. Her anguish grew to fear that she might not be able to prevent her son from ultimately being hurt by his father.

She should never have agreed to allowing Sean to do this, she berated herself inwardly, as she tried to keep awake and failed.

'Mummy's sleeping.'

Sean gave Oliver a reassuring glance as he pulled off the motorway. 'She's still not properly well.' Inside, he was more anxious than he wanted Oliver to know—and not only because of his concern that the journey might have been too much for Kate.

Perhaps it was just as well that she was asleep, he acknowledged as he drove down the familiar lanes, slowing for the small villages they passed through until finally they came to the one that was their destination.

The slowing movement of the car woke Kate, and she stared out of the passenger window, blinking away her tiredness and then freezing as she recognised her surroundings.

Accusingly she turned towards Sean, but he was concentrating on his driving as they went through the pretty little village she had sighed so ecstatically over the first time they had come here. Nothing had changed, she acknowledged numbly. Everything was still the same, right down to the small river and the main street of huddled soft stone houses with their mullioned windows.

They had reached the end of the village now, and Sean had turned, as she knew he would, up past the ancient church and along a narrow lane. A high stone wall guarded the house from her sight, but already she could see it in her memory. She felt sick, shocked, betrayed as Sean turned in through the familiar gates and the car crunched over the gravel drive.

This was the house he had promised he would buy for her; the house she had fallen so deeply in love with; the house she had talked so excitedly to him about as being the home where they would bring up their children. The house she had never lived in because he had told her that their marriage was over before she had had the opportunity to do so.

The savagery of her pain gnawed at her stomach and anger boiled up inside her. If Oliver hadn't been with them Kate knew that, however unwell she felt, she would have insisted that Sean turn the car round and take her back to her own home.

Instead she had to content herself with an acid whisper. 'I can't believe you would do something like this.'

Without replying Sean opened the car door and got out. The early-evening sun was already warming the soft cream stone of the house, and the scent of the lavender and roses filled Kate's nostrils the moment Sean opened the passenger door for her.

'I've told Mrs Hargreaves to prepare rooms for you and Oliver,' he informed Kate distantly, as he moved to help her out of her seat.

'Don't touch me,' Kate almost spat at him, hurt eyes glowing with the heat of her rage.

How could he do this to her? How could he bring her here, to the home she had thought they would be sharing? She had to swallow against the nausea in her throat.

Oliver got out of the car and danced up and down on the gravel, announcing excitedly, 'Sean, I think a puppy would like it very much here.'

'I'm sure it would,' Sean agreed gravely, but Kate could see that he was grinning, and a wave of fury swept her, making her tremble from head to foot.

'Don't you dare—' she began again, and then had to stop as the door to the house opened and a pin-neat middle-aged woman came hurrying towards them.

'I've done everything you asked me to do, Sean,' Annie Hargreaves told her employer, glancing discreetly at Kate and Oliver as she did so.

'Thanks, Annie,' Sean responded easily. 'We won't keep you any longer. I know that Bill will be waiting for his supper.'

'I'll get off, then, shall I?' she answered, turning and starting to walk away from the house.

'Annie and Bill Hargreaves look after the place for me,' Sean told Kate quietly. 'They don't live in, though—they prefer the staff quarters above the garage. I'll take you up to your room and get you settled, and then Oliver and I will bring everything in—right, Oliver?' Sean asked the little boy.

'Right!' Oliver agreed, with a worshipping smile.

Numbly Kate let Sean take her arm and start to guide her towards the house. She wanted to cry very badly but she was not going to allow herself to do so. Not now. Not ever whilst Sean was around.

The large double doors opened up onto the pretty oval

hallway she remembered, with its fairy-tale return stairway, but Kate almost faltered and missed a step as she stared around the room. She remembered it as being painted a depressing muddy beige. Now the walls glowed softly in warm butter-yellow—the same yellow she had excitedly told Sean she wanted to have it painted.

The linoleum floor had been replaced with black and white tiles, and an oval pedestal table stood in the middle of the room. As she looked round the hallway Kate started to tremble. Everything in it was just as she had told Sean she wanted to decorate it, but instead of giving her pleasure the realisation that he had opted for her choice of decor made her feel acutely sick.

As Sean studied Kate's colourless face and blank eyes, she started to sway. Cursing under his breath, he swept her up into his arms. She had always been delicate and slender, but now she felt frightening frail, he acknowledged as he ignored her husky rejection of his help and carried her up the stairs, taking them two at a time.

The rooms he had asked Annie to prepare for her and Oliver connected with one another. Kate herself had told him laughingly when they had first viewed the house that the larger of the two would make an ideal master bedroom, with the smaller one perfect for a nursery.

'The nurseries are upstairs,' Sean had told her, tongue in cheek.

Immediately she had turned her face up towards his, and, laughing, told him, 'You can't fool me, Sean. You're going to want to have our babies close to us.'

'Our babies,' he had murmured huskily. 'You know, just hearing you say that makes me want to start making them right here and now…'

'We haven't bought the house yet—and anyway there isn't a bed,' Kate had reproved him, mock primly.

'Since when have we needed a bed?' Sean had asked.

Even so she had refused to make love in the house, saying firmly that it wasn't proper since it didn't belong to them.

'I suppose that's another of those "good manners" rules, is it?' he had teased her. But in reality he had been very grateful for the tactful and loving way she had helped him acquire some necessary social polish.

When they had got home, though, it had been a different story. He had wrapped his arms around her the moment they were inside their front door, and the only sound she had made had been one of eager approval...

'Put me down—I can walk!'

Kate's fiercely independent demand told Sean that she was certainly not sharing the bitter sweetness of his sensual memories.

'Maybe you can walk,' he countered grimly. 'But on the evidence of what just happened I doubt that you could have made it all the way up these stairs unaided.'

Kate wanted to argue with him, but she was too conscious of the frantic beat of her heart. She could still remember how she had teased Sean when they had first started dating about the way he loved picking her up, accusing him of wanting to show off his superior male muscle power. But secretly inside a part of her had been thrilled by such evidence of his strength.

Now, though, it was resentment that was responsible for the rapid flip-flopping of her heartbeat, she told herself firmly, determinedly ignoring the small, conscientious inner voice that cautioned her that her resentment was desperately self-defensive.

Why should she need to feel self-defensive, after all?

she asked herself in silent bitterness. There might be a very small rebellious and unheeding part of her that was still physically responsive to Sean, but that was all. How could she, a loving and responsible mother, ever forget Sean's refusal to accept that Oliver was his son?

It was just the realisation that he had brought her here to this house—the house she had fallen in love with, had believed she would bring their family up in—that was making her feel so vulnerable, making her long to pillow her head against his shoulder and let her body relax into the comfort and security of his.

'Here we are.'

Sean used his foot to nudge open the heavy door and Kate swivelled her head to look into the room beyond it.

Sunlight warmed the soft cream walls, and wonderfully heavy curtains made of terracotta and cream toile de Jouy fabric hung from the windows, draped the antique half-tester bed. A cream carpet covered the floor, and the whole colour scheme set off the pretty late-Georgian mahogany furniture.

When Sean placed her on the bed Kate had to struggle not to give way to her emotions. The room was exactly as she had excitedly planned to decorate it, right down to the elegant cream blind at the window.

'I've had a bed put in the nursery for Oliver,' Sean was telling her practically, clearly oblivious to the emotional impact the room had on her. Had Sean converted the room next to the nursery into a bathroom, as she had wanted?

She didn't feel she could trust herself to ask, and was glad that she hadn't when Oliver came rushing in, his face alight with excitement.

'Annie says that I can go and see her dog if you say yes, Mummy,' he announced importantly.

'Annie?' Kate checked him swiftly. Sean might refer to his housekeeper and her husband by their Christian names, but Kate wasn't going to have Oliver copy his father unless he had been given permission to do so.

'Annie prefers to be addressed by her first name.' Sean stepped in immediately, reading her mind so easily and so quickly that for a moment Kate couldn't reply. 'And Oliver will be perfectly safe with her dog,' Sean continued. 'I'll take him down to meet her myself.'

Ignoring Kate, Oliver threw his arms around Sean's legs and hugged him tightly, looking up at him with an expression of beatific adoration.

Looking on, Kate could feel her heart turning over slowly and painfully inside her chest, its cavity tight with pain and love and fear.

'Can we go now?' Oliver was pleading, but Sean shook his head.

'No, not now. We'll go tomorrow morning.'

Kate held her breath warily, half anticipating that Oliver might refuse to accept what Sean had told him. Certainly he scowled, and looked as though he was about to object, but, as if he had prepared himself for Oliver's reaction, Sean simply ignored his behaviour.

'Come and have a look at your bedroom, Ollie,' Sean said instead. 'It's right here, next to Mummy's.'

Sean's use of that familiar sweet 'Ollie' made Kate clench her hands into small fists—as did the automatic way in which Sean put his hand down so that Oliver could put his much smaller one into it. Hand in hand, father and son went to inspect the room, leaving her to stare anxiously after their departing backs.

From inside the room she heard Oliver saying,

'There's plenty of room on the floor in here for your sleeping bag, Sean. You'll be able to sleep in my room, and not Mummy's.'

'Well, I'd like to do that, Oliver,' Kate could hear Sean responding seriously. 'But, you see, I have my own bedroom here—like you do at your house.'

'But I want you to sleep here with me and my mummy,' Oliver was insisting, and somehow, without knowing how she knew, Kate sensed that Sean had bent down and picked Oliver up.

'Well, when we were at your house your mummy wasn't very well, was she? And I had to be there in case she needed me. But she's much better now.'

'Well, you could sleep in the same bed, like George's mummy and daddy do,' Oliver offered, with almost-five-year-old logic that made Kate's eyes burn with dry pain.

In the room where a small child's bed had been set up for Oliver, Sean turned towards the window, the boy still in his arms. He could still feel the gut-wrenching kick of longing that Oliver's innocent suggestion had prompted.

Kate—the Kate who was no longer his gentle, loving Kathy—would never willingly welcome him into her bed. Sean knew that. Yes, on one fever-racked night when she had not known the difference between their past and their present she might have been his Kathy once again, but not in reality.

It was growing dusk and Oliver was leaning heavily against him. Reluctantly Sean remembered the emotions that had struck him when he had seen Tom go to Oliver's rescue, when he had felt irrationally that the other man was usurping his rightful role. His arms tightened around Oliver. Was the emotional bond he was beginning to develop with Oliver caused by the fact that

Oliver was Kate's child? Or was it because somehow he had begun to love Oliver for himself, to feel a fatherly love towards him?

'Why don't I put a video on for you, Ollie?' he suggested gently now. 'And then you can sit and watch it for a while before bed.'

'And then will we read Mummy a story?'

Sean ruffled the thick hair ruefully. Determined not to be accused by Kate of using the television as a babyminder for her son, Sean had instituted a bedtime ritual, aided by Oliver, of them reading a story together. Quite why he had decided that this should be done in Kate's bedroom he had no real idea, other than that he'd known how important it would be to her that she shared in her son's life in every way she could.

A small sound by the door made him turn round, and the tightening of his mouth concealed his anguished concern as he saw Kate standing there, holding onto the door itself for support.

'You're supposed to be resting,' he said curtly.

'Only when I need to, and right now I don't need to,' Kate answered evenly, refusing to look at him and holding out her arms to Oliver instead.

'Why don't I read you a story tonight, Ollie?' she suggested. 'I'm sure that Sean has lots to do.'

To Kate's shock, instead of wriggling to be set free by Sean, Oliver leaned even further into him as Sean set him on his feet.

Kate looked out through the french windows of the pretty sitting room to where Oliver was playing excitedly on the lawn with the Hargreaveses' good-natured collie dog. Child and dog were indulging in what was obviously a mutually blissful game of chase, and when

Oliver stumbled and fell on the lawn the dog was immediately all canine concern, standing anxiously over him as the little boy got to his feet undamaged.

They had been living in Sean's house for just over two weeks, and Kate was convinced that she was now fully recovered. Which meant…which meant that it was time for her and Oliver to return to their own home and their own lives.

Kate couldn't deceive herself that Oliver would want to leave. He adored Sean. Kate tensed as she saw Sean strolling across the lawn towards their son. He had left the house shortly after breakfast to attend a business meeting. The moment Oliver saw him he ran towards him, laughing happily when Sean picked him up and swung him round.

As she watched them, inside her head Kate could see another picture. In this one she was standing at Sean's side as Oliver ran towards them both, and Sean's arm was holding her close to his side whilst her head rested on his shoulder.

Her legs felt weak and her whole body was trembling—but not because she had been ill. No, she had to face up to the truth that was responsible for her physical malaise.

It seemed that nothing, not even his rejection of his son, could totally destroy her love for Sean. It was too deeply embedded within her.

Panic, anger and fear fought frantically inside her. She had to tell Sean that she wanted to leave and she had to tell him now!

Taking a deep breath, Kate went out to join them.

As he saw her approaching Sean put Oliver down.

'I'm going to take Nell home for her tea now,' Oliver

announced importantly to Kate, manfully taking a firm hold of the obliging dog's collar.

At any other time Kate knew she would have been tenderly amused, ruefully suspecting that it was the dog who was in charge of her son rather than the other away around as the two of them headed to where the housekeeper was waiting for them. But as she watched them Kate was acutely conscious of Sean coming to stand by her side. Immediately she moved slightly away from him. Letting him get too close to her was dangerous!

Bending his head, he told her quietly, 'I've been thinking there's no real reason why Oliver shouldn't have a dog of his own. In fact I called in to see a litter of Labrador pups on my way back this afternoon. They aren't quite old enough to leave their mother yet, but if you feel up to it we could drive over there tomorrow and Ollie could choose his own—'

'No! Oliver is not having a dog!' Kate stopped him sharply and Sean started to frown.

'Kate, he's desperate for one.'

'Do you think I don't know that?' Kate challenged. 'You might have been ''thinking'', Sean, but you obviously haven't thought enough,' she told him passionately. 'Surely you must realise how impossible it would be for him to have a dog at home? You know that I have to work.' Angrily she turned away from him.

'Kate—' Sean protested, putting his hand on her arm.

Immediately Kate tried to snatch her arm away, demanding furiously, 'Let go of me. I hate you touching me.'

'What?'

When she saw the expression darkening Sean's eyes Kate knew that she had gone too far. But it was too late to retract her reckless words, because he was pulling her into his hold, his arms pinioning her to his body as he looked down into her face.

'No!' Kate protested, but her denial was already being crushed beneath the pressure of Sean's angry kiss. His lips ground down on hers and his fingers tightened into the soft flesh of her arms.

Anger boiled through her veins, making her return the savage intensity of Sean's kiss. But it was an anger bred from longing and need, Kate recognised helplessly, as her own body turned traitor against her and she heard herself moaning softly with liquid pleasure beneath the demanding pressure of Sean's mouth.

Somehow the past and his betrayal of her slipped away. Without her realising it, her hands had lifted to hold Sean's face, and her heart leapt with shatteringly intense emotion. Just the slightly rough feel of his morning-shaved skin was enough to take her arousal levels dangerously higher.

Whilst her hands held Sean's face, his were moulding her body with familiar caresses, kneading her shoulders, then stroking down her spine, spanning the back of her waist and then moving lower. Kate could feel herself starting to tremble as his hands slid past her hips. His thumbs grazed her hipbones themselves, and were then withdrawn as he pulled her fiercely against his own body.

It should have been impossible for her to feel the same shockingly intense thrill of sensual arousal now, as she felt the hard fullness of Sean's erection, as she had done that very first time he had held her like this—but she did. If anything her awareness and the reaction of her body now, as a woman and not as a girl, was far more immediate and fiercely erotic than it had been then.

Perhaps it was because then she'd had no experience

by which to measure the pleasure his arousal could lead to, whereas now she most certainly did. Already her imagination had broken free of her control and was filling her head with wanton images, bombarding her senses with messages and promises that totally destroyed her defences.

Within the space of a few seconds her own body was as eager for his as it had been when she was eighteen.

The movement of his hand from her bottom to her breast evoked a low sound of delirious pleasure from her throat and she angled her body so that her breast filled his hand.

'No, Sean. No… Mmm, like that…' Kate could hear herself whispering incoherent urgent words of praise and pleasure between the frantic hungry kisses with which she was caressing his mouth. She no longer cared about what she might be revealing, only what she was feeling! 'Sean.' As she moaned his name she covered the hand he had placed over her breast with her own and whispered achingly, 'Touch me properly, Sean.'

'Properly?'

She could hear the thick male arousal roughening his voice and her skin prickled in female response to it.

'You know what I mean,' she urged him hotly. 'You know what I like.'

'You mean this?'

He was caressing the tender flesh surrounding the tormented nub of her nipple and Kate trembled violently in reaction.

'Mmm, yes. That,' Kate agreed huskily. 'And more, Sean—but without my clothes. No clothes. Just you,' she continued. 'Just you and me.'

'No clothes? Not even like this?' Pushing down her

bra, Sean used his thumb and finger to delicately rub the silk fabric of her top against the stiff thrust of her nipple.

Immediately Kate cried out in agonised pleasure.

'Good...? That was good?' Sean's voice was so thick and low Kate could barely hear it, but she didn't care. He had pushed her clothes completely aside now, and she could see the creamy swell of her breast filling the darkness of his hand as he slowly caressed her eager nipple.

Standing silently in his hold, she gave in to the violent shudders of pleasure ripping through her.

'And with your mouth...' she begged him. The words were jerked from her lips as her body suddenly convulsed against him.

'Kate! Kate!'

Just the way he was saying her name touched every one of her senses. He took hold of her hand and dragged it against his own body. Her fingers curled eagerly around the erection straining against his clothes, making a feverish exploration of their remembered territory. But she wanted to feel him without anything in the way.

She was stretching her hand towards his zip when his mobile rang shrilly, the sound jerking Kate back into reality.

What was she doing? Pulling away from Sean, she started to run towards the house, wanting to escape not just from him but also from her own self-imposed humiliation.

'Kate!'

Sean cursed under his breath when she refused to listen. The mobile was still ringing. Impatiently he switched it off, then started to follow her.

* * *

As soon as she reached her room Kate opened the wardrobe and pulled out the suitcases Sean had bought for them. Opening one of them, she started to drag clothes off the rail and throw them into it.

'What are you doing?'

The sound of Sean's voice made her swing round. 'What does it look like?' she snapped. 'I'm packing. Oliver and I are leaving! We should never have come here in the first place. I knew—'

'You knew what?' Sean stopped her.

He was looking at her with a glint in his eyes that made her heart thump and apprehension feather chillingly down her spine, but angrily Kate refused to bend.

'I know that I just don't want to be here with you, Sean,' Kate answered angrily. 'Look, I don't want to talk about it,' she threw at him when he didn't answer her.

'Less than five minutes ago you were in my arms and—'

'I've just told you I don't want to talk about it!' Kate stormed 'That…what just happened…meant nothing. It was just…'

'Just what?' Sean challenged her with a softness that was far more dangerous than anger would have been.

He was trying to make her look at him, Kate recognised, but if she did she knew he would see in her eyes how vulnerable she was. Keeping her face averted from him, she insisted stubbornly, 'Nothing!'

Something in his voice had warned her of what was to come. Panicking, Kate dropped the clothes she was holding and started to run, only realising when it was too late that—idiotically—she had run towards the bed instead of the door. Now she was backed up against it, with Sean standing in front her and no option but to turn round and try to scramble over it.

'Nice move,' she heard him say with soft amusement from behind her, and his fingers curled round her ankle as he kneeled on the bed looking down at her.

'I always did think that you've got the sexiest backside I've ever seen: nicely curved and temptingly peachy. And I can remember...'

Kate did not want to hear what he could remember, and for a very good reason. She feared that listening to what Sean could remember might make her feel even more dangerously vulnerable.

Surely there was no good reason why she should feel almost the exact same mix of nervousness and excitement lying here on a bed now, with Sean leaning over her, as she had done that very first time they had been together like this? They had been lovers; they had been married and they had been divorced—his body was almost as familiar to her as her own.

But she did feel the same, and she did feel... Stubbornly Kate tried to deny her feelings, to ignore as well the sensual caress of the bracelet of Sean's fingers round her ankle. She stiffened her body against it, just as she refused to look away from Sean when he turned his head to smile into her eyes.

'Now, about this "nothing",' he murmured, almost affably. 'Let's go through it all again, shall we? Starting right here...'

Somehow he was down on the bed beside her, the upper half of his body pinning hers to the bed, and shamingly Kate knew that a part of her was already greedily soaking up the pleasure of having him so close.

One look at his eyes told her what was going to happen. He was looking directly and deliberately at her mouth, and somehow that look was making her part her lips and wet their nervousness with the tip of her tongue.

'Nothing?' His fingertip traced the curve of her jaw and then the shape of her lips, slowly and heart-stoppingly, whilst he continued to look down at her.

'You know that I'm going to kiss you now don't you?' he whispered.

She tried to say no. She tried to mean no. But Sean was using unfair weapons against her. He knew how very vulnerable she had always been to that slow, sensual, oh-so-seductively-sweet way he had of kissing her, that made her insides melt and her lips cling to him, and the reason he knew was because she herself had told him so, over and over again, in their shared past. And maybe more recently in the heat of that fevered night? Right now all she seemed capable of doing was focusing on his mouth, whilst her heart-rate accelerated.

It had been a bad mistake to close her eyes, Kate acknowledged helplessly, a flurry of heartbeats later, because closing her eyes had somehow transformed her back into the girl she had been the first time Sean had kissed her like this.

Now, as then, her lips parted willingly and eagerly, her senses tensely aroused by the passionate intimacy of his tongue against her own, primed by the kisses they had already shared. Shockingly Kate recognised that her body was rebelliously impatient of any gentle preliminaries, that she was being consumed by a fierce, hungry surging need.

She lifted her hands to Sean's shoulders and held onto them, needing the security of their strength as her own longing smashed down on her, carrying her bodily in its fast-paced flow.

Beneath Sean's, her mouth clung and hungered, and her hands left his shoulders to press his body down harder into her own. She felt Sean tense and lift his mouth from hers to look down into her face.

Surely the hand lifted to his face, the fingers dragged sensuously against his jaw and then raised to trace the shape of his lips and run over and over his mouth could not be hers? Surely that liquid aching heat spreading through her body could be controlled if she really tried?

Surely this wasn't her, lifting her head off the bed and cupping Sean's face so that she could press impassioned kisses into his skin whilst she moaned her need softly into his mouth?

'Touch me, Sean.' *Love me,* Kate whispered silently inside herself as she stroked a trembling finger over the mouth she had just kissed. 'Make it like it used to be for us...'

Had she really said that?

'Like it used to be?' she heard Sean repeat softly. 'You mean when we were so hungry for one another that not being together was a physical pain? Is that what you mean, Kate? That you want me like that? Like this?'

As he spoke his hands were shaping her body, and Kate could feel the small flames of desire inside her, feeding on his words and growing stronger. Soon there would be a conflagration which would threaten to destroy her, and yet somehow she no longer cared about her danger—all she cared about was this, and now, and Sean's hands on her flesh, Sean's mouth on her mouth, Sean's body covering her body. The wild, untrammelled flood-force of her own dammed-up love and need crashed through the barricade, taking every single last bit of her resistance with it.

Willingly, eagerly and passionately she savoured the hot, urgent strength of Sean's kiss, meeting it and matching it just as she had done when their love was new and her faith and trust in him whole and unbroken. With her eyes closed she could even almost smell the scent of their shared past—the hot dusty air in the small suburban street mingling erotically with the fresh male heat of Sean's skin and her own excited arousal.

But the hand she lifted to curl round Sean's neck, to hold him whilst she prolonged their kiss, was the hand of the woman she was today—and today she wanted Sean as the woman she was, Kate recognised emotionally. And how she wanted him! So much, so very, very much. Her body hungered for him like parched earth crying out in silent agony for the caress of rain.

Only her need wasn't silent any more. It poured from her lips in a soft litany of longing, word on word, plea on plea, as she begged him, 'Sean—my clothes… I don't want them. I want you—your hands, your skin. You.' Kate could feel herself shuddering with the intensity of her own feelings as she twined her arms around him and her body moved restlessly against his. 'I want you, Sean,' she told him. 'The whole essence of you…all of you…'

It had always amazed her that those big, strong hands could be so delicately gentle and assured when removing her clothes, but now their unexpected impatience as Sean pulled and tugged at fabric and fastenings sent a fierce thrill of pleasure through her.

'Kate. Kate. Oh, God, how I've missed you—and this—us…'

The words tumbled thickly from Sean's tongue and were breathed against her skin as he kissed the flesh he was revealing. The sensual drift of his hands had become an urgent, compelling possession that demanded her body give itself over to him completely. The hard need of his mouth on hers spoke of a hunger so long denied that it might easily devour them both. But Kate only gloried in the realisation. How could she not when it so exactly mirrored her own feelings? The fierce thrust of Sean's tongue against her own; the heavy weight of his hand cupping the curve of her hip so possessively; the grinding heat of his body against her own—she welcomed them all.

'Take off your own clothes, Sean,' she begged him huskily. 'I need to feel you against me.' As she spoke she shuddered slightly, remembering how it had felt to have the hot satin of his skin next to her own.

'You do it,' Sean answered.

When she hesitated, he took her hand and lifted it to his body.

'Did I ever tell you how much it turned me on when you undressed me?'

When Kate just looked at him, in passion-soaked silence, he added thickly, 'Do you want me to tell you how much you are turning me on now? Do you want me to show you how much you are turning me on now, Kate?'

She was trembling so violently that she couldn't even unfasten the buttons on his shirt.

'You do it like this,' Sean said huskily, covering her hand with his own. 'And then you do this—' He guided her hand to push his shirt off his body. 'And I do this…'

Kate's whole body arched as he cupped her breast with his hand and then bent his head to cover her tight nipple with his mouth. Kate heard her own raw moan of fierce arousal as his tongue stroked the hard nub of flesh, teasing it, tormenting it. Sean seemed to know exactly when she reached the point where she couldn't bear the torment any longer, because suddenly he took the hard, wanton ache of her nipple into his mouth and drew rhythmically on it, until Kate felt as though that same rhythm was pulsing throughout her whole body, gathering deep inside her, making her want to open her legs and wrap them tightly around him.

Fiercely she tugged at his clothes and Sean helped her.

'Kate!'

The explosive denial Sean made as he virtually pushed her away made Kate stare uncomprehendingly at him.

'If I let you touch me like that I'll come too soon,' he told her rawly. 'And I don't want to do that until I've given you more pleasure than you've ever known. Until I've given you that pleasure and watched you take it from me. Until I'm inside you, where I've ached to be every single night since I've been without you. Until I've done this…'

Long, long before the leisurely journey his hands and his mouth were making over her body had reached the small swell of her belly, Kate was trembling visibly with desire.

As she felt the brush of his mouth against the soft skin of her inner thigh she closed her eyes in aching mute anticipation. His hand covered her sex, making the demanding, hungry pulse deep inside her beat faster. When his fingers parted the arousal-swollen lips of her sex she cried out loud eagerly, almost unable to bear the searing pleasure of his touch.

Her body ached and pulsed, and just the touch of his fingers against her wetness made her rake her fingers against his skin. But the eager sensual movement of her body stilled when Sean exposed the swollen, secret nub of pleasure those lips had concealed to the hungry caress of his tongue.

Kate was helpless to stop the feeling that ran through,

over her, filling her and taking her over, making her cry out and lift her body to Sean's mouth as he brought her to that place she had not known for so very long.

And then, when Sean moved and positioned himself in between her legs, taking her in his arms, Kate welcomed him with fierce pleasure. This was what she ached for—this total possession of him and by him, this hard, purposeful thrusting of him within her, that fulfilled and completed her. This climbing together towards that shimmering, shining place where for a brief heartbeat of time they were almost immortal.

Kate reached it first, crying out, her body tensing round Sean to take him with her. And as she felt the familiar pulse of his satisfaction within her Kate's eyes filled with tears.

That this act, so very, very intense and erotically a pleasure beyond all pleasures for those who loved one another, could also be the creation of life, had always given it an extra special intensity for her.

Once she had believed that Sean shared that feeling with her—he had even said that to her the first time she had shyly confided to him her deep, almost spiritual feelings about making love.

And yet now he was denying his own child!

Bitter self-loathing filled her. Where was her pride and her self-respect?

She could feel Sean withdrawing from her, not just physically but emotionally as well, and suddenly a black wave of misery and exhaustion swamped over her.

Sean looked down at the bed where Kate lay fast asleep. He had left her to go to the bathroom, and when he had come back she had been asleep. Anguish shadowed his eyes and hollowed his face as he watched her.

Whilst making love with her he had forgotten there had been another man in her life—someone man enough to give her a child. Bitterness carved his mouth into hard anger.

In his arms she had responded to him as though no other man had ever touched her, as though she had never wanted any other man to touch her… And God alone knew how much he ached and needed to believe that she hadn't. The sweet taste of her still clung to his lips, and the scent of her filled the air around him.

He couldn't endure to live without her any longer, Sean recognised bleakly. Even knowing all that he knew about her!

## CHAPTER EIGHT

KATE woke up slowly and languorously, her mouth curling into a smile of remembered bliss. Still half asleep, she stretched her body. Its telltale ache made her smile deepen. There was nothing like waking up in the morning filled with feel-good hormones, she acknowledged happily, reaching out her hand to Sean.

Sean! The speed with which she was catapulted from her warm security to stark reality physically hurt.

She sat up in the bed, her mind an agitated jumble of anxious, angry thoughts. The clothes she had been intending to pack had gone, and so too had the suitcases! The realisation that it was nine o'clock in the morning increased her agitation. It had been late afternoon when she had come up here, and...

Frantically she reined in her speeding thoughts. She couldn't believe she had slept so long and so deeply—although Sean had always teased her about it, claiming that he took it as a compliment that his lovemaking fulfilled her to such an extent.

The very words 'Sean' and 'lovemaking' linked together were making her heart thud erratically—with fury, she told herself crossly, not because of any other reason.

The sudden opening of her bedroom door brought an abrupt halt to her thoughts.

'Mummy!'

Kate's heart turned over as she looked at her son. He was wearing some of the new clothes Sean had insisted on buying for him: a pair of workman-like denim dungarees that made him look heartbreakingly grown up and yet endearingly little-boyish at the same time.

'We've brought you your breakfast,' he said excitedly.

Kate's heart plummeted at his 'we', and she prayed it was the housekeeper he was referring to, not Sean. But the tension in her stomach told her that it was Sean even before he followed Oliver into her room, carrying a heavily laden tray.

'You've been asleep for a very long time,' Oliver reproached her, and then beamed from ear to ear. 'Mummy, I made your toast—and my daddy helped me…'

All three of them froze, and above and beyond her own anguish Kate was seared by the look in Oliver's eyes, his face scarlet as he ran to her and clambered onto the bed, burying his hot, embarrassed face against her body. Automatically she wrapped her arms protectively around him. Unlike Kate, he was too young to recognise why he had called Sean his daddy, but he was not too young to know that he should not have done.

Over Oliver's downbent head Sean looked at Kate, and he put down the tray in silence before turning to leave.

It couldn't be put off any longer, Kate told herself fiercely. Her heart had bled drops of pure concentrated emotion for her son, his betrayal of his feelings and his need, but Oliver's innocent indication of the role he longed to have Sean play in his life had hardened her resolve to leave.

It filled her with a pain like no other she had ever known to recognise her son's vulnerability. How much unintentional damage had she already done by letting him know Sean?

She was well aware of the old cynical saying that it was a wise child that knew its own father. But what if somehow, somewhere, unknown to modern scientists, there was a primitive, instinctive bond between father and child that had been activated by Sean's appearance in Oliver's life?

The feelings she had experienced at Oliver's realisation of his *faux pas* in calling Sean his 'daddy' went way beyond tears. Of course she had pretended not to be aware of the cause of Oliver's crimson face and discomfort, had coaxed him to share her toast and to tell her about the previous afternoon's activities, when the housekeeper had let him play with the dog and then given him his tea.

But even that had been a mistake, Kate reflected unhappily. Because Oliver had gone on to tell her that Sean had collected him from the housekeeper's quarters, brought him back, given him his bath and read his story to him.

'D— Sean said that you were very tired and needed to sleep.' Oliver's innocent comment had torn at her heart as Kate had acknowledged just why she had 'needed to sleep'.

But even worse than that had been the longingly hopeful look in Oliver's eyes when he had looked up at her and told her, 'I want to stay here for ever, with Nell… and with Sean…'

Kate's heart had sunk when he had suddenly avoided looking at her.

'Well, it has been very nice here,' she had agreed, trying to sound calm. 'But what about George? He's your friend and—'

Oliver had stopped her stubbornly. 'Sean is my friend, and so is Nell. A dog can be a friend, and Nell is mine!' And had completely defeated her when he had added, 'I wish that Sean was my daddy.'

Now, from the sitting room window, she could see Oliver industriously helping the gardener to 'weed'. Helplessly she closed her eyes against her own pain.

When she opened them again she could see Sean's reflection in the glass beside her own. Immediately she turned round.

'We need to talk,' Sean told her flatly.

'There's nothing to talk about.' Kate stopped him bitterly. 'I've almost finished packing, and—' Unable to stop herself, she said quickly, 'I know you must think that I primed Oliver to…to say what he said. But I didn't. He sees George with Tom and… He…he's had this bee in his bonnet for a while, about not having a father…'

Sean recognised that the new name she had chosen for herself suited her. She was Kate now, a woman. Not Kathy, a girl. And he knew that there was something about Kate that he responded to as a man. Kathy the girl had gone, and it grieved him to know that this maturing process had taken place without him being there to share in it. And if that grieved him how the hell was he going to feel if she spent the rest of her life apart from him?

'I've got a proposition to put to you,' he said curtly. 'Or perhaps I should more properly say a proposal,' he amended heavily into the silence that followed his initial words.

'A proposal?' Kate tasted the word cautiously, her stomach churning. What was he going to do? Offer her money to take Oliver away and deny that he was his father? 'What kind of proposal?' she challenged him suspiciously. The look he was giving her was decidedly ironic.

'I thought you knew, Kate, that in my world there is only one kind of proposal a man makes to a woman the morning after they have spent the night together. Anything else *would* be a proposition.' When she went rigid and simply stared at him, he elucidated tiredly, 'I am asking you to marry me, Kate.'

The shock ran through her like lightning, a vivid flash of disbelief followed by an unbelievably intense and coruscating pain, out of which she could only demand sharply, 'Why?'

'Why? Because I want you back as my wife, and—' Sean turned his head and looked out across the lawn, his face averted so that Kate could not see his expression as he added emotionlessly, 'And because I want Oliver as my son.'

It was, Kate decided, almost as though she was hearing Sean speak from very far away, through an impenetrable glass wall.

The angry and rejecting words, *But Oliver is your son* rolled like thunder through her heart, but somehow she managed to hold them back. And she held them back because inside her head she had a painfully clear image of a small boy who desperately wanted a father. If she knew anything about Sean she knew that he was a man who committed himself totally and completely to everything he decided to do—almost single-mindedly so at times.

She had seen for herself the rapport he was developing with Oliver, and she knew that to pretend such a bond was simply not in Sean's nature. But she could not and would not take risks with her son's emotional future!

'Your son?' she questioned coldly 'But, Sean, you

have already refused to accept that Oliver is your son. You have told me that you believe another man fathered him, and, believing that—'

'That isn't a road I'm prepared to go down.' Sean stopped her sharply. When he saw her face he demanded savagely, 'Don't you realise how it feels for me to know that there's been another man in your life? In your bed? Didn't last night tell you anything about how much I still want you? The only way I can deal with this is to draw a line under it, Kate, to box it up and bury it somewhere so deep that it can never be disinterred.'

'Do you think it's any different for me? You were unfaithful to me, Sean.'

'You can forget all about her, Kate. She never really—'

'Meant anything to you?' Kate stopped him bitingly.

Sean looked away from her. He had almost fallen into the trap of saying that the other woman had never really existed!

What would Kate think if she knew the pitiful, pathetic truth about him? How would she react? Would she pity him? Reject him? Would knowing the truth enable her to understand how deeply and completely he loved Oliver and wanted to be a father to him?

A part of him yearned to share his knowledge and his pain with her, but his pride held him back.

'Oliver needs a father,' he said heavily instead. 'And I—'

'You want to take pity on us?' Kate suggested angrily, reluctant to admit even to herself just how strongly his impassioned words had touched her emotions.

'No,' Sean denied, the glimmer of ironic self-mockery glinting in his eyes, concealing his pain. 'I want you and Oliver to take pity on me.'

It was as close as he could bring himself to telling her the truth.

When she didn't answer he told her bleakly, 'Both of us know how it feels to grow up without the love of a parent. Oliver wants a father.'

Kate couldn't stand any more. The words *Oliver has a father* burned on her lips, but in the garden she could see her son, and already she knew how much it would mean to him if she agreed to what Sean was suggesting. 'I—I...' As she tried to squeeze out her denial all she could hear was Oliver calling Sean his daddy.

She might be able to resist all the emotional pressure that Sean could possibly put on her, but no way could she resist that special sound she had heard in her son's voice.

She took a deep breath. 'Very well. I accept. But if you ever, *ever* do anything to hurt Oliver I shall leave you there and then,' she warned him passionately.

She had already turned away from him when she heard him coming after her. As she stopped moving he took hold of her, imprisoning her in his arms whilst he kissed her with fierce passion.

Helplessly Kate felt her mouth softening beneath his, and her traitorous body, still flooded with sensual memories of his lovemaking, simply softened into his until she was moulded against him so closely that she might have been a part of him. He might have started the kiss, but she was the one who prolonged it, Kate recognised hazily as her mouth clung to his, and she gave in to her need to trace the shape of his mouth with her tongue-tip and to slide her fingers into the thick darkness of his hair.

Against her body she could feel the hard pulse of his erection. Mindlessly she pressed closer to it, waiting for

Sean to cup her breast with his hand and discover the hard eagerness of her nipple. But instead he pushed her way from him, breaking the kiss.

Humiliated, she was about to walk away from him when she heard him saying in quiet explanation and warning, 'Oliver!'

It shocked her to realise that Sean had been more aware of their son's approach than her, but her hope that Oliver had not witnessed their intimacy foundered as he stepped through the open french window and immediately demanded, 'Why were you kissing Sean, Mummy?'

Before Kate could think of anything to say, Sean answered for her, telling him calmly, 'We were kissing because we are going to get married, and that's what married people do.'

As he finished speaking Sean kneeled down and held out his arms to Oliver. 'I've asked your mummy to marry me, Oliver. And now there's something I want to ask you.' Kate couldn't help it; emotion welled up inside her. But it was nothing to what she felt when Sean continued, 'Will you let me be your daddy, Oliver?'

The look on Oliver's face as it lit up with delight was all the answer he needed to give—that and the fact that he threw himself bodily into Sean's arms!

As Sean stood up, hoisting Oliver onto his shoulder, the little boy was chanting, 'Daddy—Daddy. I can call you Daddy now, can't I, Sean?'

As Sean nodded his head Kate was sure she could see the glint of moisture in his eyes.

## CHAPTER NINE

SEAN had insisted on a church ceremony, much to Kate's surprise, and even more surprising was just how very much like a new bride she actually felt, standing in the doorway of the small church ready to walk down the aisle to where Sean was waiting for her.

The graceful dress she was wearing was cream, the heavy satin fabric rustling expensively as she turned to look down at Oliver. 'Ready, Ollie?' she asked him tenderly.

He had been so excited about today, but now that it was here he looked round-eyed and slightly over-awed.

John was going to give her away, but it was Oliver who was going to walk down the aisle with her. That had been her decision, and one that Sean had listened to in shuttered-eyed silence.

Inside the church, with the heat of the sun shut away, the timelessness of this place where people had worshipped century upon century cast its own special grace over them as Oliver reached up and slipped his hand into hers.

Together, as the sound of the organ music surged and swelled, mother and son walked towards the man waiting for them, and into whose care they were giving themselves.

They had almost reached him when Oliver tugged on Kate's hand and announced in a loud stage whisper, 'Mummy, I'm really glad that Sean is going to marry us.'

Kate completed the last few steps in a blur of tears, totally overwhelmed by her emotions.

The artfully simple bouquet of lilies and greenery she carried were removed from her by Carol, but when her friend went to take Oliver's hand, to lead him away, Sean shook his head and took it himself.

Then, with Oliver standing between them and both of them holding one of his hands, the vicar began the service that would reunite them, bind them not just as husband and wife, but this time as parents as well.

'Okay?'

As the bells pealed in celebration of their marriage and the sun shone down Kate nodded mutely. Surely she wasn't still brooding on the perfunctory kiss with which Sean had acknowledged his new commitment to her, was she?

She had remarried him because he was Oliver's father, and not for any other reason, she told herself fiercely.

Their wedding breakfast was being held in a private dining room at a very exclusive local hotel, and from there they were flying to Italy for a few days. Initially she had tried to protest, but Sean had overruled her, announcing that the three of them needed time together alone, away from their normal environment, to start establishing their new roles in one another's lives.

Of the three of them, Oliver had certainly had no difficulties whatsoever in adapting. The word 'daddy' seemed to leave his lips with increasing regularity. In fact she could hear him saying it now, as he beamed up at Sean and told him importantly that he was now his little boy.

A small shadow touched Kate's face.

'I want to adopt Oliver legally,' Sean had told her abruptly the previous week.

Kate had refused to respond. How could he adopt his own son?

Kate opened her eyes reluctantly, unwilling to abandon the dream she had just been having in which she had been lying in Sean's arms, their naked bodies entwined. The huge bed in their hotel suite was empty of her husband, though. Last night, following their arrival, when she had seen the suite, she had unwisely exclaimed, 'Are we all in the same room?'

'I thought you'd prefer it that way,' Sean had responded.

'Yes. I do,' Kate had agreed, but she knew that a tiny part of her couldn't help comparing the circumstances of this, their second honeymoon, to the first one they had shared. Their surroundings might not have been anything like as luxurious, but even the air in the small room had been so drenched with the scent of their love and hunger for one another that it had been an aphrodisiac all on its own.

That had been then, though, and this was now!

And where was Oliver? The small bed Sean had insisted on having set up in their room was also empty.

Anxiously she pushed back the bedclothes and reached for her robe. They'd arrived so late in the evening that she had done no more than nod in acceptance of Sean's description of their suite and its facilities, but now, as she pushed opened the door onto their private patio, she caught her breath in delight.

The hotel had originally been a small palace, and their suite was at ground level for Oliver's benefit. From the patio Kate could see the still blue water of the hotel's breathtakingly effective infinity pool. The sound of splashing water to the side of her caught her attention, and she froze as she realised that it was Oliver who was causing it, and Sean stood at his side in what was obviously a children's swimming area, encouraging him to swim.

Encouraging him to swim! But Ollie couldn't swim. She had done everything she could to get him to swim, right from him being a baby, but he had steadfastly clung on to his terror of the water. Until now… Until Sean…

Out of nowhere a feeling she just did not want to analyse struck her. She felt excluded, unwanted. She felt jealous, Kate recognised, angry with herself for having such feelings.

Sean had told her that he wanted to remarry her because of Oliver, but suddenly it was striking her exactly what that meant.

Sean had always wanted a son, and now, as a very successful businessman, no doubt he wanted one even more. Given his own childhood, Kate could see that creating his own dynasty would appeal to Sean. But that did not mean that he loved Oliver—and it certainly didn't mean that he loved her.

Had she done the right thing in marrying Sean? Or had she given in to her emotions? Hadn't there been somewhere deeply buried inside her a small, desperate hope that somehow Sean would come to recognise that Oliver was his son and that in doing so he would…?

He would what?

She could hear Oliver and Sean making their way back. Quickly she pushed her anxiety to one side.

The moment they walked onto the patio Oliver ran

towards her, shouting excitedly, 'Mummy—Mummy, I was swimming.'

As he launched himself at her Kate caught him up in her arms, closing her eyes as she savoured the echoes of his babyhood in the smell of his skin and its softness.

'I can't believe you haven't taught him to swim,' she heard Sean commenting grimly, and he reached out and took Oliver from her arms with the automatic action of a man who knew it was his right to hold his child.

Kate held her breath, telling herself fiercely that it wasn't disappointment that filled her when Oliver went happily to Sean.

'I tried.' She answered Sean's criticism defensively. 'But right from being a baby Ollie has been frightened of water...'

'Well, he isn't frightened now,' Sean announced. 'Shower now, Ollie, and then breakfast,' Kate heard him saying firmly as he put Ollie down.

Once he was out of earshot Sean said, 'Perhaps he could sense that you were afraid for him? Children need to feel that they are safe.'

'Thanks for the child guidance lecture,' Kate snapped furiously. 'But I'd just like to remind you, Sean, that I've been Oliver's mother from the moment he was conceived.'

'And I am now his father,' Sean replied fiercely.

They were words which were constantly inside her thoughts and her heart over the following few days of their brief 'honeymoon', as Sean and Oliver formed a close male bond from which she felt totally excluded.

And now, with their holiday over, Kate couldn't help observing as they walked towards Sean's parked car that Oliver was even beginning to talk like his father.

Mrs Hargreaves was waiting to welcome them when they arrived home, and although Kate was vaguely aware of the conspiratorial look the housekeeper exchanged with Sean, she didn't pay very much regard to it, or to the few private words she hurried to have with Sean.

Upstairs, she was turning to head for her bedroom when Sean stopped her.

'I've asked Mrs Hargreaves to move your things into the master bedroom.'

Kate's stomach muscles quivered. Angry with herself for the fierce stab of pleasure the thought of sleeping with Sean again caused her, she forced herself to object. 'But that's your bedroom.'

'It was my bedroom,' Sean agreed coolly. 'But it's now our bedroom.'

Their bedroom. The unwanted feeling intensified and spread. Kate knew that she was perilously close to giving in to her renewed love for Sean. He might want her sexually, but he had told her himself that he had remarried her for Oliver's sake.

She wasn't going to humiliate herself by offering him a love he didn't want!

How long, though, would she be able to keep her feelings to herself if she was sleeping with him every night and all night?

'I don't—' she began.

'Not in front of Oliver,' Sean checked her firmly, leaving her to wait to resume their conversation once Oliver had been introduced to and safely established in his own new bedroom.

'That was ridiculously extravagant, Sean, buying him a computer games console,' Kate protested when Sean had finished showing Oliver how to operate his new toy and they were back on the landing outside his room.

'It will be good for his spatial dexterity,' Sean told her without a glimmer of contrition. 'Come and see how the master bedroom looks,' he added, guiding her to the door.

The first thing Kate saw when he opened it was the huge new bed. And her concentration remained stuck on it.

'It's a double bed!' she pronounced foolishly.

'King-size, actually,' Sean corrected her dryly.

Panic filled her. Double or king-size, it didn't really matter. What mattered was that she would be sharing it with Sean and she knew, just knew, it would be impossible for her to stop herself from snuggling up to him and allowing herself the luxury of behaving as though they still were the loving couple they had once been.

Blindly she swung round, and then found that her exit from the room was blocked by Sean's arm, Sean's hand holding the door—a door which he promptly closed and leaned against, folding his arms as he watched her furious agitation.

'I can't sleep in that bed with you!' Kate burst out.

'Why not? We shared a room when we were away!'

'That was different!' Kate insisted, wishing he wouldn't give her that look of slow, deliberate scrutiny that made her feel he could see right into her head.

'We are married, after all,' Sean reminded her. 'And besides, the bed's plenty big enough for us to keep our distance from one another, if that's what you want!'

'Of course that's what I want,' Kate lied quickly. He couldn't have guessed how much it affected her to think of sleeping in the same bed with him, could he?

'We've got to think of Oliver,' Sean told her firmly.

'What kind of impression is it going to give him if we have separate rooms?'

She had been outmanoeuvred, Kate recognised, unable to do anything other than retaliate furiously, 'I saw the look Mrs Hargreaves gave you when we arrived, and now I realise why,' she accused him wildly.

To her surprise her comment seemed to have a more powerful effect on Sean than she had anticipated, because he suddenly started to frown, and a look she couldn't translate shadowed his eyes.

'I've told Mrs Hargreaves that from tomorrow we'll both have a light tea with Oliver at five o'clock, and then our own dinner later on, when he's in bed. I think it's important that we share his mealtimes with him. And I thought I'd take him over to the farm tomorrow—the pups are almost ready to leave their mother, and Mrs Hargreaves has told them we're going to have one. Ollie can choose his own.'

It was nine o'clock at night. Oliver was already tucked up and fast asleep in his new bed, and she and Sean were eating the delicious meal Mrs Hargreaves had left ready for them before going home. Suddenly the last thing Kate felt like was eating.

'Since when did you and Mrs Hargreaves make arrangements concerning Oliver without me being informed?' Kate demanded ominously. As she spoke she stood up, throwing down her linen napkin and gripping the table in her fury.

'He's desperate to have a dog of his own,' Sean told her. 'You know that!'

'I also know that I said I didn't want him to have a puppy yet.'

'Because he would be at nursery and you would be

working. That doesn't apply any longer,' Sean pointed out firmly.

Kate was shaking with a mixture of anger and misery without really knowing why—other than that it had something to do with that large master bedroom and its huge bed, in which she and Sean were going to sleep—with most the bed between them...

'I'm not listening to any more of this,' she told Sean angrily, pushing back her chair and almost running out of the room, ignoring his pleas to return.

'Kate! Come back!'

Idiotically, it was the master bedroom she headed to for refuge, swinging round white-faced as Sean followed her into it, shutting the door.

'What's got into you?' he demanded.

'I've managed to spend five years bringing Oliver up without your assistance and without your interference, Sean. I am his mother...and I—'

'And you what?' Sean challenged her savagely. 'And you shared another man's bed in order to conceive him?'

The raw emotion in his voice shocked through her. She had never seen him so out of control, and the intensity of his unexpected outburst paralysed her.

'Do you think I don't think about that every single day, every damned hour? Hell, Kate, do you think that because I can't father a child, because I'm not man enough to father a child, I'm not man enough to think about you and him and this?' Silently they stared at one another.

Kate drew a ragged breath and demanded shakily, 'What do you mean, you can't father a child?'

Her mouth had gone dry and her heart was thudding in heavy, erratic hammer-blows. Even through her own shock she was aware of the look of sick, anguished despair in Sean's eyes, and she could feel the intensity of his pent-up emotions.

When he started to turn away from her she reached out and took hold of his arm.

'You are Oliver's father, Sean,' she said quietly.

'No, I'm not. I can't be,' Sean denied bitterly. 'I can't father a child. It isn't medically possible.'

'I don't understand,' Kate said in a dry whisper as she struggled to take in what he was telling her.

It was too late for him to backtrack now; Sean knew that. Behind the shock he could see in Kate's eyes he could also see a growing determination. He knew she would insist on being told the truth—and what point was there in hiding it now, after what he had just said?

He took a deep breath.

'At a routine annual check-up for my private medical insurance the doctor suggested that I might as well have the full works.' He gave a small bitter shrug. 'It was just a formality, or so I thought—just a means of putting on paper what I believed I already knew. That I was a healthy, fully functioning man. When the results came back there was a problem...'

He paused and Kate waited, aching with compassion for him, but with the sure knowledge that, no matter what he had been told, the experts had got it wrong. He had fathered Oliver.

'It seemed—he said... He told me that my sperm count was so low it would be impossible for me to father children,' he said bleakly. 'I refused to believe him at first. In fact I was so convinced he must be wrong that I demanded that they run the tests again. They weren't wrong!' He closed his eyes. 'Shall I try to explain to you, Kate, how savagely humiliating I found it to have to stand there and listen to the doctor telling me that I wasn't capable of giving you a child? How I wished I hadn't heaped fresh humiliation on myself by demanding they re-run the tests?'

'Why didn't you tell me...say something?' Kate demanded in a dry whisper.

'I couldn't,' Sean said bleakly. 'I couldn't bear to see your face when I told you that I couldn't give you the children I knew you wanted so much.'

*So much,* Kate wanted to tell him. *But never, ever more than I wanted you, Sean.* She knew what he was like, though. She knew how deeply such news would have cut into him, into everything he'd believed about himself.

'I had a right to know, Sean,' she told him quietly.

'And I had a right to protect you from knowing,' he countered.

'To protect *me*?'

Sean's mouth compressed. 'I knew if I told you you would insist on...on accepting that there could never be any children for us and...and sacrificing your own chance to be a mother because of that. I decided there and then that I wasn't going to let you do that, and that I...I had to set you free to find another man to...to give you what I could not.'

'To set me free?' Now that she was over her initial shock Kate was beginning to get angry. 'You were unfaithful to me, Sean, and—'

'No!'

'No?'

'There wasn't anyone else. I...I just made it up because...because I knew how you would feel and how you would react. I didn't want to keep you trapped in our marriage, sacrificing yourself to it for my sake, pitying me and eventually hating me for what you were being denied. I must say, though, that I didn't expect you to find someone else quite so quickly. Was that why it didn't last?'

A lump had lodged in her throat and she could only shake her head in helpless denial. She didn't know what was hurting her the most—her pain for Sean or her pain for herself.

'Sean, I don't care what the medical reports said. Oliver is your child,' she told him passionately. 'Sometimes such things are possible and—'

'No!' His harsh, haunted cry made her flinch.

'Don't offer me that kind of temptation, Kate. You are worthy of so much more than deception, and so is Oliver.'

Kate went white, but before she could defend herself he was continuing rawly.

'Can't you understand how I feel? How much I wish that Oliver could be mine? How much it hurts me that he isn't? I only have to look at him, never mind hold him, to feel my lo—something here inside me that… Having children with you, giving you our children, was so deeply rooted in me, so instinctive, that I thought I could never endure knowing that another man had given you what I couldn't. I thought it would drive me quite literally mad to see you with another man's child. But—'

'Oliver *is* your child,' Kate protested emotionally. 'He is yours, Sean—ours…'

'Don't do this to me, please, Kate. I can't bear it! What do I have to do to stop you lying to me? This?'

Kate couldn't move when he took hold of her, the fierce pressure of his mouth on hers bending her head backwards against the hard strength of his arm. The heat of their emotions, anger on anger, welded them together, and sent a shaft of pure molten reaction speeding through Kate.

How could it be that such a fierce primeval desire could be born out of anger? Her whole body shook in recognition of her vulnerable naïveté. She hadn't recognised her danger and tried to evade it. It was too late now.

She was held in thrall, emotionally and sexually, as much to the intensity of her own surging need as she was physically to Sean's iron-armed imprisonment of her.

When he broke the kiss, lifting his mouth from hers, his chest rising and falling quickly, Kate tried to pull away from him. But Sean refused to let her go.

'Perhaps the only way I can stop thinking about it is to put my own sexual imprint on you, for ever.'

'You were the one who divorced me, Sean,' Kate reminded him, trying to free her senses from the effect his hot, turbulent gaze was having on them, and at the same time fighting frantically to stem the excited surge of liquid sexual longing that was pulsing through her.

'I may have divorced you but I didn't replace you in my bed, Kate,' he answered her bitterly. 'How much did you want him?' he demanded rawly.

'Sean! No!' Kate protested, torn between shock and pain—shock that he could actually believe she had given herself to someone else when he knew how much she had loved him, and pain for him, for herself, because he did.

'No? You didn't say no to him, did you?' he challenged her thickly. 'I'm going to make you forget that you ever knew him, Kate. I'm going to make you want me so much that you'll forget he ever existed.'

Sean was already caressing the side of her neck with

his lips, deliberately seeking the special place where, she had once confessed shyly to him, feeling his mouth made her melt with longing for him.

'Did he do this?'

The words muffled against her skin made her throat ache with agonised suppressed tears, her only response a mute shake of her head.

'You didn't tell him how much it turns you on?'

There was an ugly note in Sean's voice that spiked her heart with angry pain. To her own shock, despite her anger, she ached to be able to reassure him, to convince him that no man ever had or ever could take his place in her life. In either her life, her heart, or her body. But the words wouldn't come, despite Sean's angry assault on her senses.

'Did he touch you like this, Kate? And like this?'

The angry, destructive words hammered into her like blows, numbing her body and freezing her emotions. A cold emptiness was spreading inside her, squeezing the life out of her love with icy binding tentacles of rage that stiffened her body into furious rejection.

'Oh, God, Kate.'

The groaned, anguished words were expelled with so much force that she could feel their pressure against her skin.

Releasing her, Sean went over to the bed and sat down on it, his elbows on his knees as he dropped his head into his hands.

'What the hell am I doing?'

The suffocating anguish of his pain filled the space between them.

With his head bent over his hands, she could see how exactly like Oliver's his hair grew, Kate noticed. For some reason that knowledge made her take a tentative step towards him.

'What the hell's happening to me? I know I've always been a jealous bastard where you're concerned, but—'

The muffled words bled shocked despair.

Kate lifted her hand and placed it on his head.

Immediately his whole body froze.

'For God's sake, Kate, don't touch me. How can you touch me?' he demanded savagely.

As his hand moved Kate saw the telltale moisture on his face and her heart turned over with love and compassion. An extraordinary feeling of strength and understanding filled her. Reaching out, she placed her hand over his.

Immediately Sean pushed her hand away and stood up, in rejection of her touch.

'I'll sleep in one of the other rooms tonight,' he said stiffly.

As he started to walk away from her Kate saw the way the light falling against his thigh revealed the swell of his arousal, and something inside her, something elemental and untamed, reacted to it.

Quickly she stepped in front of him, looked up into his face.

'No more, Kate,' Sean told her wearily. 'I don't want—'

'This?' She stopped him, placing her lips against his and caressing them slowly and sweetly, letting her senses and her heart revel in self-indulgent pleasure as she did so. She felt the involuntary movement of his body as he tensed it against her, but she wasn't going to give in.

'Or this?' she whispered against his mouth, sealing it

with her own as she let her hand drop to his body so that her fingers could stroke possessively against him.

He didn't respond for so long that she was almost on the point of giving up, and then suddenly and explosively the power was taken from her and he was returning her kiss—not angrily, but passionately, hungrily, as though he was starving for her.

Just as she was starving for him?

Somehow, some way, somewhere, the anger between them had taken another direction, had pushed through the barrier of her self-protection and found that place deep within herself where she was still the girl who loved Sean and responded to his lovemaking with eager, open passion.

She could feel that passion flooding through her now, taking her to a place she had thought lost to her for ever.

Clothes tugged and pulled by impatient fingers left a trail to the bed, where they stood body to naked body. Kate's arms wrapped around Sean's neck as she continued to kiss him with fierce female hunger.

'Kate!'

She felt his hands on her breasts, holding and shaping them, and she shuddered, racked by fierce tremors of pleasure at his open appreciation of their soft weight in his hands. A wild wantonness had entered her blood and taken her over. As she was now taking him over! It manifested itself in the hot sensuality of the way she kissed him, touched him, the way she subtly and deliberately encouraged and invited him, winding her arms around him, pressing her naked body against him, driven by a force she could neither control nor deny.

A force she didn't want to control or deny, Kate recognised with feverish arousal, and she slid her hands down Sean's torso and through the soft thickness of his body hair, stroking over the hardness of his erection and then curling her fingers around the hot swollen shaft, caressing it slowly and then more urgently whilst the tension seated deep inside her own body tightened and ached until she knew it could not be contained any longer.

Sean! As she held out her arms to him Kate let the top half of her body drop onto the bed.

The last of the light was fading across the bedroom, but there was still enough left for her to see Sean's expression, to watch the way his glittering gaze was drawn to her body, over the firm swell of her breasts, over her nipples, dark rosy peaks of open arousal. The last glow warmed her belly and highlighted the soft little curls decorating the swollen mound that signposted her sex.

Deliberately she opened her legs, and watched the shudder that racked Sean's body.

Briefly she gave in to the temptation to stroke the wetness of her own sex, watching the way Sean's gaze followed her small erotic movement, and then blazed with heat. A fierce spiral of female excitement ran through her.

'You do it,' she told him boldly.

And, as though he knew what she was feeling, Sean groaned and reached for her.

Possessively Kate wrapped her legs around him, moaning her pleasure as he touched her just as she had wanted him to do, replacing his fingers with his body when he realised how close she was to her orgasm.

Within seconds it was over, her climax so immediate and so intense that her womb actually ached with its aftermath.

Her womb!

Bright tears glittered in her eyes and she turned her

head away so that Sean couldn't see them. Once she would have taken that fierce clenching of its muscles as a sign that it was claiming the seed of life Sean had planted there, but Sean refused to believe that he could give her a child.

# CHAPTER TEN

'READY, then?' Sean asked curtly, not looking directly at Kate herself as he strode into the sitting room, but crouching down instead to hold out his arms to Oliver, who immediately ran into them.

He had been like this with her—cold, distant and rejecting—ever since the night they had made love. If he had written them out in ten-feet-high letters he could not have made his feelings plainer, Kate admitted unhappily.

He might share the large bed in the master bedroom with her, but he slept with his back to her, and the cold space between them might as well have been impassable snow-capped mountains. His whole body language told her he didn't want her anywhere near him.

And why should he? In his eyes he had got what he wanted out of their marriage, after all, Kate acknowledged bleakly, as she looked down at her son and her husband.

'You don't have to take us to the hospital, Sean,' Kate told him now. 'This check-up is only a formality. The doctor said that himself, and I already know that I'm fully recovered.'

'I thought you said you wanted to check on your house?'

'Yes, I do,' Kate admitted. 'I know that the letting agent says he's found someone who wants to rent it right away—'

'You'd be better off selling it,' Sean interrupted her grimly.

Now it was Kate's turn to look away from him. How could she explain to a man in Sean's enviable financial position how she felt about the small home she had worked so hard to buy? And how could she tell him there was a part of her that was afraid that somehow history might repeat itself, that she might find herself on her own and in need of the security her little cottage could provide?

'I prefer to keep it,' she answered him.

'I spoke to my solicitor yesterday,' Sean announced, standing up. 'About the adoption.'

Oliver was running towards the door, but even so Kate gave Sean a warning look—which he obviously misinterpreted. As Oliver hurried out to the car Sean's face hardened.

'In your eyes I might be Oliver's father, Kate, but in my own eyes I am not—so I want to make sure that I am in the eyes of the law, for Oliver's sake as much as my own.'

Too heartsore to make any response, Kate followed him out to the car.

They had stopped off on their way to have some lunch, and now Sean was parking his car outside the doctor's surgery.

'There's no need for you and Oliver to come in with me, Sean,' Kate said as she opened the car door, but she might as well have saved her breath.

Not only did Sean insist on waiting with her to see the doctor, he also insisted on going into the room with her.

'I can understand your husband's concern,' the doctor further infuriated her by saying placatingly. 'You were very poorly.' He shook his head. 'Yours was certainly the worst case of this virus I have seen.'

'Perhaps she should have a full medical—with heart and lung checks?' Sean suggested.

'Sean, there is nothing wrong with me,' Kate told him angrily.

'Mummy was sick after breakfast!'

In the silence that followed Oliver's innocent but revealing piece of information all three adults turned to look at him.

'I…it was the red wine I had with dinner,' Kate explained uncomfortably.

Immediately the doctor's expression relaxed, although he did tell Kate warningly, 'Red wine can sometimes prove too strong for a delicate stomach.'

'You barely touched your wine last night,' Sean pointed out as they left the surgery.

'Because I wasn't enjoying it,' Kate returned quickly.

To her relief he didn't pursue the matter. Instead he said, 'We might as well leave the car here and walk to your house. It isn't very far.'

Automatically Kate fell into step beside him, with Oliver in between them.

Perhaps the walk was too familiar to her, or perhaps her mind was on other things—Kate didn't know which, but obviously her concentration wasn't what it should have been, because when Oliver pulled his hand free from hers and shouted out the name of his friend she didn't react as quickly as she could have done. Oliver had run into the road before she had realised what was happening.

She did see the huge lorry bearing down on him, though, and she did hear her own voice screaming out his name in anguished terror as she started to run towards him, even though she knew she would be too late.

There was a blur of movement at her side as Sean ran past her and into the road, grabbing hold of his son in a rugby tackle movement, covering Oliver's body with his own.

Kate heard Oliver's screams and the hiss of air brakes. She could smell the odour of burning rubber, taste her own fear in her mouth. The lorry had slewed to a stop and people were running into the road to stand over the still, crumpled figure lying there.

But Kate got there first.

Sean lay motionless on the tarmac, blood oozing from a cut on his head, one of his legs splayed out at a sickeningly unnatural angle. And, lying safely next to Sean's unconscious body, Kate could see Oliver, his eyes wide with shock as he whimpered, 'Daddy…'

There were people everywhere—the doctor…sirens… an ambulance…

Hugging Oliver tightly to her, Kate got in it—after the paramedics had carefully lifted Sean onto a stretcher and placed him inside.

His face was drained of colour and Kate had to fight back the sickly sensation of wanting to faint as one of the paramedics expertly set up a drip and started to check his vital signs.

'His body's in shock, love,' one of them said, trying to comfort Kate as she stared at him in anguish. Unable to stop herself she took hold of one of his hands. It felt icy cold—as though…

Her heart lurched against her ribcage, her gaze going fearfully to the heart monitor.

'Hospital's coming up now. And we've got one of the best A&E departments in the country here,' the friendly medic told her proudly. 'Good timing, too. We've still got over half the golden hour left.'

'The golden hour?' Kate questioned numbly.

'That's what we call the window we get after an accident—leave it too long and—' As he saw Kate shudder he checked himself and looked uncomfortable, realising he had said too much.

In Accident and Emergency a nurse took Oliver from Kate's numb arms whilst Sean was rushed past them on a trolley.

'I want to go with him—' Kate began, but the nurse stopped her firmly.

'We've got to get him ready for the duty surgeon to see him. You wouldn't want to watch us cutting off those good clothes he's wearing, would you? Now, let's have a little look at this young man, shall we?'

Distractedly, Kate tried to focus on what she was saying.

Miraculously Oliver had sustained little more than some grazes and bruises—no, not miraculously, Kate recognised. Because Sean had risked his life to save him.

A huge lump rose in her throat. Sean was right. It did take more than fathering a child to be a father, and he had proved that today. And he had proved, too, just how much he loved Oliver.

The medical staff were kind, but nothing could really alleviate the anguish and fear Kate experienced as she waited to hear how Sean was.

To her horror, a neurologist had to be called in to examine Sean and check for brain damage.

An hour passed, and then another. Oliver fell asleep in her arms and Kate's eyes prickled dryly with the weight of her unshed tears. After what felt like a lifetime, a consultant strode into the waiting area and came across to her.

Numbly Kate focused on the spotted bow tie he was wearing. 'My husband?' she begged anxiously.

'He's sustained a broken leg, and some cuts and bruises, and for a while we were concerned that the bump on his head might turn out to be rather nasty.' When he saw Kate's expression he gave her a kind look. 'Fortunately it's nothing more than a bad bump, but we had to make sure. I'm sorry that you've had to wait so long, but you'll understand that we had to be certain...'

Tears of overwrought emotional relief were pouring down Kate's face.

'We've had to mess him around rather a lot, and we've had to operate on his leg. We've still got a few samples to take, but he's fully conscious now. He won't accept that his son—Oliver, is it?—is all right until he has seen him. Susie will take you through,' he told Kate kindly, waving a hand towards a nurse waiting next to him.

But Kate didn't move. She couldn't. An idea...a hope...was burning on her tongue.

'The samples you have to take,' she began in a fierce rush. 'Would you—could you...?' Taking a deep breath, she told him helplessly, 'Sean won't believe that Oliver is his son, but he is. If you could do a DNA test—'

The consultant was frowning. 'That would be most irregular.'

'Sean already loves Oliver,' Kate told him desperately. 'He risked his own life to save him.'

'How sure are you that the child is his?' the consultant asked bluntly.

'Totally sure,' Kate answered him.

'I'm afraid that I can't do as you ask without the patient's permission,' the consultant told her, adding quietly as her face fell, 'However, I believe it is possible to have such tests conducted via certain Internet Web sites, should a person deem it necessary to do so.'

'But how—?' Kate began helplessly.

'All that is required is a small sample—a snippet of hair, for instance.'

Kate swallowed hard. 'You think I should…?'

'What I think is that anyone doing such a thing should be guided by their own conscience,' the consultant told her seriously.

Biting her lip, Kate turned to follow the nurse down the corridor.

Sean was in a small private room, surrounded by a heart-stoppingly serious-looking battery of medical equipment, and when Kate saw the 'bump' on his head the consultant had referred to she almost cried out loud.

It looked as though the side of his head had been dragged along the road—which it most probably had, she acknowledged shakily.

'Look, Sean, we've brought Oliver to see you, like we promised,' said the nurse.

As Sean turned his head Kate had to fight the compulsion to hand Oliver to the nurse and run to his side, to take Sean in her arms.

How could such a big man look so frail? Her heart turned over as she whispered his name—but Sean wasn't looking at her. His whole attention was concentrated on Oliver.

'Daddy!' Oliver exclaimed, suddenly waking up and holding out his arms to him.

'Give him to me,' Sean demanded in a hoarse croak.

Uncertainly Kate looked at the nurse, who nodded her head briefly. Gently Kate carried Oliver over to the bed, but instead of handing him to Sean she sat down on the bed next to Sean, keeping hold of Oliver, afraid that her son might inadvertently hurt his father.

'He's all right?' Sean asked Kate as he lifted his hand and touched his son.

'He's perfectly all right—thanks to you,' Kate replied, her voice trembling.

It wasn't Oliver she wanted to hold and protect right now, she recognised achingly, it was Sean himself. But she knew that he wanted neither her comfort nor her love.

'Gently, Oliver,' she protested automatically as Oliver leaned forward to give his father a big smacking kiss.

'There's no need for you to keep visiting me twice a day like this, Kate,' Sean announced curtly as Kate opened the door to his private room.

Suppressing her hurt, Kate forced herself to smile. 'Mr Meadows says that you'll be coming home tomorrow.'

Sean frowned.

'Oliver can't wait,' Kate told him.

Immediately the frown disappeared.

'He's been pining for you, Sean.'

Ruefully Kate decided that she wasn't going to tell him what she had done to try to alleviate her son's longing for his father—he would discover the new addition to their household for himself soon enough. Kate had to admit that she had been pleasantly surprised at how quickly Rusty, as Oliver had decided to call his new puppy, had become housetrained.

'Did you get the neurologist to check that absolutely no damage had been done when he…?'

Every time she visited him Sean demanded to know how Oliver was, and even though she kept telling him that he was fine he still persisted in worrying. Kate suspected that he wouldn't be reassured until he was home and could observe Oliver's excellent and boisterous good health for himself.

'I spoke to my solicitor this morning,' he announced abruptly. 'He says you're refusing to sign the adoption papers.'

Kate poured herself a glass of water from the jug at Sean's bedside in an attempt to quell the feeling of nausea the hospital smell was giving her.

'I'm not refusing, Sean, I...' Crossing her fingers behind her back, she said quickly, 'Your adoption of Oliver is such an important and...and special thing, I didn't want it to be purely businesslike and clinical. I thought if we waited until you came home we could have a little celebration.'

'So it isn't because you're having second thoughts, then?' Sean cut across her hesitant excuse.

The temptation to tell him emotionally that the only time she could have had second thoughts about his role as Oliver's father had been nine months before Oliver's birth was something she had to stifle before she could give it voice.

Deep down inside she still felt guilty about that little snippet of hair she had cut from his head whilst he had been sleeping. As the consultant had hinted, she had found a Web site offering the kind of service she had needed and Sean's hair, together with a lock of Oliver's, had been sent to it. She had no doubts, of course, as to the result she would receive back.

Automatically her hand dropped to her stomach and rested there.

So far as Sean's accident was concerned, the consultant had told her cheerfully that she was worrying for nothing, that Sean was a fit, healthy man with a skull thick enough to protect him from its contact with the road and a broken leg that was healing extremely well. But Kate knew that as long as Sean was here in this hospital she would continue to feel that he was vulnerable and needed to be treated with care.

Dry-eyed, Sean watched Kate leave. He had had time and more to spare during these last few days to think. And he'd had plenty to think about. The past and the future.

The present situation was a warning to him of how the people who mattered most to him were precious and yet so vulnerable. *All* that mattered to him, Sean acknowledged fiercely, was Oliver, the child he had come to love with a true father's love, and Kate, the girl he had loved, the woman he still loved, beyond and above anything and everything that had happened or might happen.

Oliver and Kate. He couldn't bear the thought of losing either of them. Even in that half-second as he'd recognised Oliver's danger he had known that it didn't really matter that he hadn't fathered him, or even that there had been another man for Kate. That was the past. He had their present, and he wanted their future.

'So, no playing football with that leg, and come back for your check-up in six weeks,' the consultant told Sean breezily as he gave him his final examination before discharging him. 'You'll be looking forward to getting home to your wife and son,' he added easily, but he was watching Sean as he spoke.

Following Kate's request, he had sent for and checked all Sean's medical records. One of them recorded a specialist's opinion that it would be a miracle if Sean ever managed to father a child.

'You were damn lucky not to be much more seriously injured, you know,' he commented. 'But then, as we in the medical profession are often forced to accept, miracles do happen!'

Sean closed his eyes. He wasn't going to dispute what the consultant was saying; after all, he had his own private, secret miracle to rejoice in.

Five years ago, if someone had told him that there would come a day when he would not only accept another man's child as his son but he would love that child more deeply than he had ever imagined he could or would love anyone, apart from Kate, he would have denied it fiercely and immediately. But that was how he felt about Oliver.

When he had seen the little boy standing in the path of the lorry he had known that he loved Oliver as fiercely and protectively, as deeply and instinctively as though he were his biological father. Oliver was his son, and he loved him as his son. But legally Oliver was *not* his son, and if for any reason she chose to do so Kate could simply take Oliver and walk out of Sean's life with him.

Any reason? Sean's mouth compressed. Kate had a very good reason to want to leave him, and he had given her that reason that night they'd made love...

It made no difference to Sean's contempt and disgust for himself that ultimately mutual passion had flared between them. His only excuse was that his pent-up jealousy had overwhelmed him, and that was no real excuse at all. He loathed himself for what he had done, and he knew that Kate must loathe him as well—for all that she was concealing it.

The door to his room was opening. A smiling nurse came in, and behind her were Kate and Oliver.

When Oliver broke free of Kate's hold and ran towards him Sean bent his head over Oliver's to conceal his emotions.

'He refused to wait at home for you,' Kate explained as Sean picked up the crutches he would need to use.

Immediately Kate was at his side, but Sean refused to let her help, turning away from her.

White-faced, Kate watched as the nurse went to Sean's aid…Sean's side…taking the role which should have been hers. Sean might have remarried her, but he didn't want her as his wife, Kate acknowledged bleakly.

'I've asked Mrs Hargreaves to move my things into one of the other bedrooms.'

Kate was glad she had her back to Sean, so that he couldn't see her reaction to his words, although she couldn't stop herself from demanding, 'But what about Oliver? You said—'

'I've told him that it's because of my leg,' Sean answered her curtly.

But of course that was just an excuse, and Kate knew it! He didn't want to share a room with her, a bed with her, any longer—because he didn't want her!

They were standing in the hallway, Sean leaning on his crutches whilst Oliver chased his puppy around the room, trying to catch him so that he could show him to his father.

'I see you changed your mind,' Sean commented sardonically as he looked at her.

'I'm a woman. I'm entitled to,' Kate replied as lightly as she could. There was, though, another reason she had decided that this was the optimum time to allow Oliver to have his puppy.

Had Sean recognised the pup as being the one he himself had picked for Oliver? she wondered. If he had he didn't make any mention of it, and ridiculously, after everything else that told her how he felt about her, she felt absurdly disappointed and hurt.

'I'll help you upstairs,' she offered, going to his side. But immediately Sean stepped back from her in such an obvious gesture of repudiation that Kate froze, then turned round so that Sean wouldn't see the humiliating tears burning her eyes.

## CHAPTER ELEVEN

NAUSEOUSLY Kate put her head back on the pillow and closed her eyes. Perhaps it was just as well that Sean was not sharing the room with her.

Sean!

It was Sean's birthday today. She reached for the packet of dry biscuits she had bought herself earlier in the week, when she had bought his birthday card.

She took her time getting up, waiting for the nausea to subside before going in to Oliver.

He was as excited as though it was his own birthday, Kate acknowledged ruefully as he collected the present they had wrapped together so carefully the previous day.

Sean was already sitting in the breakfast room when they went in, and immediately Oliver ran over to his father and scrambled onto his knee, shouting, 'Happy birthday, Daddy!'

Bending her head to hide her own emotion, Kate picked up the card Oliver had dropped in his excitement, reflecting that it was just as well she had carried the present for him.

'Happy birthday, Sean,' Kate echoed more sedately, adding, 'And it's a double celebration now that your plaster cast is off!'

He had had the plaster cast removed the previous day, and the consultant had expressed himself totally satisfied with the way the leg had healed.

'I've got you a card and a present!' Oliver exclaimed importantly, still sitting on Sean's lap.

Obediently Kate handed over the card and the present.

'You've got to open this one first—it's my card,' Oliver instructed. 'Mummy has a card for you, too, and so does Rusty. He's put his own paw mark on it,' Oliver told him excitedly. 'Mummy made some special mud, and we put his paw in it, and then we put it on the card!'

'Some special mud? That sounds clever!'

Was that really a gleam of amusement she could see in Sean's eyes as he looked at her? Kate's heart somersaulted inside her chest.

'That explains the odd marks on Mummy's jeans yesterday, then, does it?' he added dulcetly.

'We did have a couple of aborted attempts.' Kate laughed, but when she looked at him Sean wasn't sharing her laughter. Instead he was looking at Oliver's card. And he continued to look at it for a several seconds, before lifting his head and looking at Kate.

'Do you like it, Daddy?' Oliver demanded, tugging on his arm.

'I love it, Ollie!' Sean assured him gruffly. 'But I love you even more.'

As he hugged him he put the card down and Kate reached for it, standing it up on the table. Oliver's writing wasn't very good as yet, but his message to his father was: 'I love you lots, Daddy.'

'And you've got to open my present now,' Oliver insisted.

Kate watched as Sean unwrapped the photograph she had taken of the two of them and had framed. As Sean studied it she held her breath. Could he see, as she had, the likeness between them?

If he could he obviously wasn't going to say so.

The rest of the cards were opened, including the one from Rusty. Then Sean assured Oliver gravely that he was indeed looking forward to his birthday tea, and eating the cake Oliver and Kate had made for him.

Kate said nothing.

'Mummy, you haven't got a present for Daddy,' Oliver piped up suddenly.

'Yes, she has, Ollie,' Sean told him, before Kate could say anything. 'Your mummy has given me a very, very special present—the best present in the world.'

'Where is it?' Oliver asked him, bewildered.

Over his head, Sean looked at Kate. 'You are it,' he answered. 'Your mummy has given me you.'

Kate knew that she should have been thrilled to hear Sean's words of love for Oliver, and of course she was, but a part of her ached with pain because she knew that they confirmed what she didn't want to hear: that Sean only wanted her because he wanted Oliver.

That was not the kind of relationship she wanted with the man she loved, the man who—

Abruptly, she got up.

She had left her gift for Sean in the room he used as an office. When he found it he would realise that in order to have Oliver he did not need to have her as well.

'Kate, where are you going? You haven't eaten any breakfast.'

She didn't turn round.

'I'm not hungry,' she answered, and instinctively her hand went to her stomach.

Not hungry? Sean wondered bitterly as she walked away. Or not able to endure his company?

As soon as they had finished their breakfast, Sean took Oliver out into the garden, along with the puppy. Did Kate even realise she had picked the same pup he had chosen?

As they walked side by side Oliver chattered happily

to him, and when he looked down at him Sean felt a stab of pain for the years of his life he had missed, for not being there at his birth. His large hand tightened around Oliver's smaller one. Oliver was his son, but he had not been entirely truthful when he had said that Oliver was the most precious gift he could have been given.

He was precious, very precious, but Kate's love was just as precious. There hadn't been a night since it had happened when he had not lain awake, hating himself for the way he had treated Kate. No wonder she couldn't bear to be in the same room as him.

It was lunchtime before he went into his office and saw the large white envelope lying on his desk.

Frowning, he picked it up, recognising Kate's handwriting on it,

'For you,' she had written, 'and for Oliver.'

Still frowning, Sean opened it. Removing the contents, he read them, and then read them again. And then again, trying to focus through the blur of his own shocked emotions.

He had fathered Oliver. It was here in black and white. The incontrovertible proof in their DNA records.

He read them again, and then again, over and over, until finally it sank in that there was no mistake.

*Miracles do happen,* the consultant had told him, and now Sean knew that it was true! But his miracle had come at a dreadful price, he recognised as the reality of what the results meant sank in.

He had refused to believe that Kate had not slept with another man. He had done so much more than refuse to believe her…

He heard the office door open.

Kate walked in and closed the door. She looked at the desk, and then at him.

'So you've opened it?'

'Yes. But I wish to hell that I hadn't!'

Kate felt sick. What was he trying to say? 'But it proves that Oliver is your son!' she protested.

'Oliver was already my son!' Sean told her harshly. 'Here in my heart was all the proof that I needed or wanted—even if it took a near tragedy to make me realise that. Kate! This—' he told her, furiously picking up the results, 'means nothing!'

Kate was too shocked to speak.

'I want Oliver to grow up knowing that my love for him comes from here,' he told her, as he touched his own heart, 'and not from this!' Angrily he threw down the piece of paper. 'I had a lot of time on my hands to think whilst I was in hospital, Kate, and what I thought, what I learned, and what I finally accepted was that love—real love—should and can transcend all our weaker human emotions. Jealousy, doubt, fear. I love you as I have always loved you,' he continued thickly. 'As the only woman for me. My other half, who I need to complete me…my soul mate. Nothing can change that. Nothing and no one. And I love Oliver as the child of my heart.

'This…' he gestured towards the test results '…underlines the fact that I haven't just abused you and your trust once, but twice. That I have created yet another barrier between us with my own selfishness and stupidity.'

Dizzily Kate looked at him. 'You love me?'

Sean frowned, caught off guard not just by her question but by the exultant pleasure that lightened her voice.

'You want me to?' he demanded.

'Oh, Sean!' Tears blurred her vision as she took a step towards him, and then another, until she was close enough to wrap her arms around him. 'Always and for ever. You and your love.' Emotion choked her voice and she shook her head. 'If you love me, why have you been rejecting me? Why have you—?'

A tide of colour began to creep up under Sean's tan.

'I thought—I felt… That night when we made love… God, Kate, do I have to spell it out for you? I lost control and I—'

Gently Kate placed her fingers against his lips to silence him.

'We both lost control, Sean, and as a result of that…' She paused. 'Do you really mean this, Sean? Do you really love me?'

'How could you even ask?' Sean groaned as he pulled her closer and kissed her downbent head.

'Well, it isn't just for myself that I have to ask,' Kate answered slowly, trying to pick her words as carefully as she could.

It was obvious to her when he put his hand under her chin and tilted her face up towards his own so that he could look into her eyes that he hadn't grasped what she was trying to say.

'You mean because of Oliver?' he asked her, puzzled. 'You know I love him.'

'No, not because of Oliver,' she told him. 'But you're on the right track.'

Encouragingly she looked at him, until he made a smothered sound and bent his head to take the softness of the half-parted lips she was offering to him.

Their kiss lasted a long time and said a great deal, promising love and commitment and sharing sadness and regret, but eventually it ended, and Sean demanded rawly, 'You can't mean that you're pregnant?'

Kate gave him a quizzical look. 'Who says I can't?' she teased flippantly, before giving a small shrug that didn't quite manage to conceal her excitement.

'Apparently modern research has shown that a woman's body has the capability to fight hard to receive and cherish the sperm of the man she loves—and after all, Sean, it only takes one!'

Tenderly Sean drew his fingertip down the curve of her cheek. 'Well, this is certainly not a birthday I'm going to forget.'

'Mmm, and it isn't over yet,' Kate reminded him softly, adding naughtily, 'You know how women get cravings for things when they're pregnant…?'

Dutifully, Sean nodded his head.

'Well, my craving is for you, Sean,' she told him gently. 'And besides, you don't want your baby to think you don't love her mother, do you?'

'*Her* mother?' Sean questioned softly, several hours later, as he propped his head on his hand and looked down into Kate's face.

Her mouth was curved in a smile of warm, sensual satisfaction whilst her eyes glowed with love and happiness.

'Well, I think she's a girl,' she answered him lovingly, before adding, 'It's because of the pregnancy that I got Ollie his puppy now. One baby at a time is enough for any household!'

'Oh, God, when I think of what I could have lost. What I did lose in those hellish years without you,' Sean said, drawing her back into his arms and nestling her against his body. 'Thank you for forgiving me for what

I did, for making it possible to have you and Oliver in my life.'

'Once I understood why you had done what you did, it changed everything—especially when I saw the way you were bonding with Ollie. Of course I hated the fact that you were refusing to accept that Oliver was your child, but from a logical point of view I understood why you'd refused to believe it. And I never stopped loving you, even if I didn't like admitting it!'

'Well, from now you aren't going to be allowed to stop loving me,' Sean told her softly. 'And I am certainly never going to stop loving you.'

# EPILOGUE

'I THOUGHT you said that one baby at a time was enough?'

Kate gave Sean a rueful look and they both looked at the two perfect and identical babies sharing the same hospital cot.

Their daughters had been born within ten minutes of one another earlier in the day, and after bringing Oliver to see his new sisters Sean had taken him home and put him in the care of Mrs Hargreaves before returning to the hospital to be with Kate.

'I thought you said it was impossible for this to happen!' Kate responded, and then felt her eyes moisten with ridiculous emotional tears as she saw the male pride in Sean's eyes battling with the awareness that Kate had done the hard work of carrying and giving birth to them.

From the moment they had known Kate's pregnancy was twins Sean had worried anxiously over her, but now…

Gently Sean reached for her hand and carried it to his lips. 'Without you this wouldn't have been possible,' he told her emotionally. 'You could have fallen in love and had your children with another man, Kate. But somehow I know that my problem would have made it impossible for me to father children with anyone but you.'

Of course she ought to tell him that he was being silly, but she wasn't going to, Kate decided. No, what she was going to do was to cherish this moment for the rest of her life.

'I see Rusty has managed to send one of his unique paw-print cards,' she murmured teasingly. 'Three paw-prints, too, and two of them pink!'

Sean laughed. 'I've got a confession to make,' he warned her. 'The creation of that card involved the destruction of several items of clothing and Annie Hargreaves threatening to leave! But Oliver was insistent! Fortunately the lure of the twins was enough to make her change her mind!'

The babies were waking up and would soon be demanding a feed, Kate knew. But there was still time for her to lean forward and show their father how much she loved him, and she placed her lips to his.